LAST
FLAG
FLYING

Darryl
Ponicsán

sphere

SPHERE

First published in the United States in 2005 by The Wright Press
Reissued and revised by Skyhorse Publishing in 2017
First published in Great Britain by Sphere in 2017

1 3 5 7 9 10 8 6 4 2

Copyright © Darryl Ponicsán 2005, 2017

The moral right of the author has been asserted.

*All characters and events in this publication, other than those
clearly in the public domain, are fictitious and any resemblance
to real persons, living or dead, is purely coincidental.*

A CIP catalogue record for this book
is available from the British Library.

ISBN 978-0-7515-7180-6

Printed and bound in Great Britain by Clays Ltd, St Ives plc

Papers used by Sphere are from well-managed forests
and other responsible sources.

Sphere
An imprint of
Little, Brown Book Group
Carmelite House
50 Victoria Embankment
London EC4Y 0DZ

An Hachette UK Company
www.hachette.co.uk

www.littlebrown.co.uk

To Tom Wright

LAST
FLAG
FLYING

Postmortem

MULE COULD ARGUE THAT HE saw Billy Bad-Ass dead. He witnessed, more or less, the Shore Patrol take his pulse, and he heard it said, "This bad ass is dead," or words to that effect, words hard to misinterpret. He would swear that is what he saw and heard, though he was at that time and place unforgivingly drunk. Still, he could make the argument, if ever it came up, but for thirty-odd years it never did, and although the detail stays fresh in his mind, Billy Bad-Ass is now just another name and an indistinct visage among hundreds, thousands of half-remembered shipmates from fourteen years as a sailor. Fourteen years, nine months, if you count the brig time, which he does not.

Wolfe, who should have been the barracks authority, since he drew the TDY of escorting Billy's body back home to Pennsylvania, never returned to Boston to tell the story. From Pennsylvania, he inexplicably was ordered on to San Diego and put on an aircraft carrier. He spent the next nine months cruising the South China Sea. By the time he resurfaced in the world the legend had run its course and had become a half-believed cautionary tale for chasers upon being issued their side arms, a duty that never fell to Wolfe. Had he returned to the transit barracks as he was originally supposed to he would have told them that what he escorted to Andoshen, PA, was not the body of Billy Bad-Ass but that of an eighteen-year-old quartermaster striker named John Pennypacker, who had succumbed to spinal meningitis, one of three that week, setting off a small panic and an 0400 wake-up for inoculations all around.

As for Meadows, a key player before the fact, or what was believed to be the fact, he spent the whole eight years on the shelf.

When Meadows thought about Billy Bad-Ass and Mule Mulhall, which was often since he had few life experiences to refresh the stagnant days, he pictured them together at sea, their true element, deporting themselves honorably, Mule the gunner's mate running tests on the ship's armament; Billy the signalman up on the bridge, flashing messages across the water. He saw them standing inspections on deck and being commended by the captain. He saw them enjoying liberty in foreign ports, Billy working his devilish smile on the girls, Mule acting cool. Near the end of his stint in the brig, he imagined them mustering out. Cashing in on unused leave time. Going someplace nice for R&R before settling into civilian life and second careers. In his mind, he always saw them together. Old shipmates.

One

BILLY BAD-ASS IS ALIVE! And living—where else?—in Norfolk, Virginia. Shit City. It might as well be home, it occurred to him thirty-four years ago when he was told to go home. The place was in many ways livable. It never got too cold or too hot, and when the fleet went out there was always an abundance of suddenly available women.

With each decade since leaving the Navy the signalman has gained a permanent ten pounds, but they fit him well and he remains a person to be approached with caution, unless you come in from the right side. He has constant pain in that shoulder and has difficulty raising his right arm above shoulder level. His prostate is enlarged, and his sleep is broken by the need to get up and pee. He has a prescription for that which Medicare doesn't cover and he doesn't always take. Other than that, he is in good shape for a man his age. He can't run, but these days finds little need for it.

He manages his own little bar, Billy B's Bar 'n Grille, in a neighborhood where sailors used to go on liberty but don't anymore. The bar is small and dark and unprofitable, but it makes Billy a businessman, and that designation in some perverse way pleases him. The ceiling is festooned with insignia caps of ships based in Norfolk, many now decommissioned, and of those ships that have passed through, whose crews found their way to Billy's bar and left at least a cap, at most some blood on the floor. It is decor enough. There is one coin-operated pool table, owned and maintained by the psycho son of an aging gangster, and an ancient jukebox still spinning vinyl. Its most recent addition, and probably the least played, is "Join the Navy" by the Village People. A string of Christmas lights twinkles behind the bar. It's been there for years. Billy plugs it in the day after Thanksgiving and unplugs it on New Year's Day. The bar itself is short, seating only seven along its longest part, then three more where it takes a forty-five-degree turn, then another two where it takes another forty-five-degree turn and abuts to the wall. This is the section Billy dryly calls "The Reservation Desk," because the telephone is there, as well as a stack of cocktail napkins and a goblet of matchbooks, their covers blank because he has lost his contract with Camels. Now out of spite he sells only Luckies and American Spirits, neither of which give him little more than spit. The wood of the bar, well worn, reveals a rich pattern of grain that can cause dizziness among those of little restraint who sit at it for too long. Three booths and half a dozen tables complete the place.

It is now a Saturday evening on a chilly December. Billy leans on his elbows on his side of the bar, doing the crossword. He sometimes whiles away the time playing cribbage, but you need another person for that and, really, four-handed is best. Recently he discovered the solitary pleasure of crosswords, hearing that it helps stave off Alzheimer's disease. He solves one daily. He smokes a Dominican cigar, chewing its end more than it needs. He wears a cropped mustache, going gray like the sides of his short-cropped hair, which he has trimmed twice a month at Supercuts. While working on crosswords, he wears glasses, Navy issue, left behind years ago by some customer too drunk to remember.

At the other end of the bar, a TV set hangs suspended. *Cops* is on. Billy's only customer, O'Toole, who used to be quite the gambler in his day, which is long past, is watching a young couple nervously trying to explain to a sarcastic cop what they are doing in the Projects if not buying drugs.

O'Toole laughs at the wit of the arresting officer, but the whole exercise annoys Billy.

"Drug users and johns," Billy says, "just people hurtin', tryin' to find a little pleasure in life, I ask you: you ever see these cops catch a killer on this show?" The question is rhetorical. "You ever see them catch a bank robber, even? You ever see them bring in a CEO of a big corporation? Heads 'n' johns. Without them there'd be little need for cops."

"What have you got against cops?"

"Nuttin'. What I got against is stupidity."

O'Toole lets it go. He nurses his beer and watches his favorite TV show.

Outside and across the street, a man in a heavy windbreaker stands idly. He wears a watch cap. You can see his breath. An AWOL bag is on the sidewalk at his feet and a garment bag is slung over his shoulder. He is looking at Billy's place and doing nothing more than that, looking at the window. You would have to know him well to realize that he is smiling. The window of

Billy B's Bar 'n Grille displays two semaphore flags. This man happens to know semaphore. The red triangle, white background is Foxtrot. The red-and-white squares is Uniform. Foxtrot/Uniform. Fuck you. Good old Billy Bad-Ass.

Of all manner of men, the easiest to identify on sight must be the Sad Sack. The Sad Sack appears incapable of having a good time, which is not necessarily true, but your idea of a good time is not his. Lined up shots of Jagermeister, sassy girls with bare and pierced bellies, crowded dance floors, and spectacular sound systems give him no joy. In fact, seen alone in the midst of all these stimulants, and alone is his usual state, he becomes an object of ridicule to you and to your circle of laughing friends.

The man watching Billy's bar is a Sad Sack, even while he is smiling, and, again, you wouldn't know he was smiling.

Someone looking at him curbside might assume that here is an unhappy man who has lost his way. Somewhere else, a person might stop and offer to help him find it again, but in this neighborhood lost people are left to their own devices, which are few.

It is not the eight years of hard time in a Marine brig that have rendered him permanently blue. Simply, it is his way. If anything, the brig put him in a state of suspension that he sometimes misses.

* * *

O'Toole doesn't care. He will, like anyone else, look up when the door opens, but long ago he lost interest in who comes and goes. As proprietor, however, Billy automatically does a quick assessment of anyone entering his establishment, especially on a slow night, which lately all of them have been. This one is transient, but not a permanent transient, because he has a garment bag, which means he is carrying a suit. He's foot traffic, waiting for a cab, looking for an address. What's with the watch cap? Maybe an ex-swabby covering some old haunts. Doesn't go with the suit, even though the suit is still under wraps.

The man hangs his garment bag on a hook on the stanchion and takes a stool. He puts his AWOL bag on another stool. He settles down with a little uncertainty, as though already a bit regretful he isn't closer to the TV or that he is here at all. He looks into his wallet and withdraws a ten-dollar bill and lays it on the bar.

Billy puts down his pencil, says, "What can I get you?"

"Beer."

"What kind of beer?"

"Any kind."

"Draft or bottle?"

"Draft."

This is the kind of customer who can annoy Billy. Doesn't know what he wants. Guy goes into a bar, doesn't know what he wants. . . . And now the dude is smiling, like there's something funny about it. Am I going to have trouble here?

(The clue here is that Billy can see he is smiling.)

Billy serves him the beer, takes the money, makes the change, and goes back to the crossword.

Four-letter word for "Bean Curd." Doesn't have a clue.

The man takes a swallow and says, "Good beer."

"It's from Pennsylvania."

"You must be Billy."

"That I am."

"How long have you had this place?"

Is this dude just making small talk, or what's he after?

"Too long," says Billy.

"It's real homey."

"Yeah? Where do you live?"

"New Hampshire," says the stranger, not catching Billy's wit. "Ever been there?"

"Once. I've been everywhere once."

"The B is for Bad-Ass, am I right? Billy Bad-Ass."

Billy still doesn't look up from his crossword. "That's affirmative," he says.

"How do I know that?"

"Somebody told you."

"Maybe. Sailors come in here on liberty, huh?"

"Not anymore."

"How come not?"

"They want music, they want drugs . . ."

"I don't blame them."

"Neither do I."

The stranger takes another appreciative swig of beer and looks into the glass, thinking, out loud after a minute:

"There's port 'n' starboard liberty. There's Cinderella liberty . . . there's stick liberty. . . . Those are the liberties."

"There's long-glass liberty," says Billy.

"Long-glass liberty? Never heard of that one."

"You woulda, if you was in Panama with me in the early sixties. Tied up in port and restricted to the ship, fifty-two days, because of the riots. Hot? You could dehydrate just lyin' in your rack. The sweat would roll from your nose to your shoulder and down your arm right off your fingertips. You'd go up on the bridge and grab a telescope and try to catch some local girl with her clothes off. Oh, joy. That was long-glass liberty."

"I never got to do sea duty."

"Be grateful."

"Cinderella liberty is when you have to be back by twenty-four hundred hours."

What is this dude, writing a book?

"And stick liberty is Shore Patrol duty."

"You know the lingo."

"You ever been on stick liberty?"

"Been on *all* of 'em, all over the fuckin' world. Permanent liberty is the best. Or maybe the worst. I haven't decided."

"I like this bar. It's homey."

"You said that."

"I was a sailor once."

"I figured."

"For only a little while."

Billy looks up at him. For only a little while?

"Yeah? Where was that?"

"Here. Norfolk. Boot camp at Great Lakes, then here, then . . . you don't remember me, do you?"

Now Billy takes the time to look him over. Everybody expects you to remember them, even when they never did anything memorable. These days he can't even remember half the women he's fucked, and that's just the ones he didn't have to pay. He takes off his eyeglasses. His eyebrows come together. He squints, as though that eliminates all ambiance, and focuses on the subject. Then his eyebrows go up and the cigar hangs down. The shock of recognition.

"Can't be," he says.

"Could be," says the other.

"No way."

"Way."

"Sweet Jesus . . . the kid?"

"Not anymore. Nobody's called me kid in a long, long time."

"Fuck me . . . you made it."

"Yeah. No problem."

"No shit, you made it. Good on you, kid. You look great. You here to kick my ass?"

"Huh?"

"O'Toole! This is the kid. Remember the kid I told you about?"

"What kid?"

"The kid I chased to the brig that time."

"What time?"

"Listen up, why don't you? They fucked him over with eight years and a DD for rippin' off the PX for forty bucks."

"Ah, yes, the unfortunate kleptomaniac. I didn't know you meant that kid."

"He's gonna kick my ass now."

"Well deserved. I'll hold his coat."

"I am not," says the stranger who is now being called kid.

O'Toole is already back into his program. A skinny black man whose fat white wife is kicking *his* ass, regularly.

"The one true exploiter of the black man," O'Toole observes, "is the fat white woman."

"I ain't kicking anybody's ass."

"I'm just kiddin'," says Billy. "I'm a troublemaker."

"Still?"

"Naw."

"Besides," says Meadows, "you could probably kick *my* ass."

"Probably."

"He flatters himself," says O'Toole. "No one else does."

"And you shut up before I kick *your* ass," Billy tells O'Toole.

"Yeah, yeah, yeah," says O'Toole, watching the TV.

"You gotta excuse me, lad, I forget names."

"It's Meadows. Larry Meadows."

"Meadows! Right. Seaman Meadows, busted down to E-1. It's been a long time."

"Over thirty years."

"Hasn't been that long."

"Yes, it has. Thirty-four years."

"No."

"Yeah, it has. Since you and me 'n' Mule . . ."

"Mule. Right. Gunner's mate. Good sailor. Have another beer. On the house. Fuck, I'll have one with you."

"How is old Mule?"

"I wouldn't know. I ain't seen him since that day."

"You haven't?" Meadows is surprised and saddened. He thought they would always be friends.

"Naw. It all went way wild after that, as I recall."

"What do you mean, wild?"

"Well . . . just, uh . . . we didn't know what we were doin', man. We got all turned around, and the end of the story is, we wound up not runnin' into each other after that. Drink played a part."

Meadows smiles again. He does.

"A big part," says Billy, "because I don't remember much."

"So you don't know whatever happened to Mule?"

"No, not on my list of concerns. Dudes come 'n' go, especially in transit. You go out on details . . . you get orders . . . you do your job, you go your separate ways . . . though that one was a lulu. It turned out to be my last detail."

"It did? You got out of the Navy right after that?"

"Yeah, kind of a negotiated settlement. And it's never been the same since. The Navy, I mean."

"I'm a little . . . shocked."

"Why's that?"

"I thought you were a lifer."

"Me? Fuck no. I never took a solemn vow to spend my life in the Navy. Oh, wait a minute . . . yes, I did."

He pours two beers and sets them down, even though Meadows has hardly touched his first.

"Welcome back, lad . . . Meadows."

They clink glasses and drink.

"It's good to see you again, Billy."

"Likewise, I'm sure." Though Billy has a feeling that the kid is no happier now than he was the last time he saw him, with a cage closing behind his back. Mule could see that right away, as soon as they started the detail. The kid couldn't have a good time, he said, it wasn't in him.

"But, dammit, kid, we had a good time, didn't we? We had some fun."

"Yeah, we had a lot of fun those few days."

"We did. We had fun, the three of us."

"We sure did. I laugh sometimes when I think about it."

"You do?"

"Sometimes. A little."

"You got to," says Billy. "You got to laugh at everything. I laugh at my fuckin' prostate gland, laugh in its fuckin' face. I laugh every time the doc gives me a finger wave. Fuck it. Laugh at it all."

"How do you do that?"

Billy gives some thought to it. "Dunno," he says.

"You're lucky you know how. I don't know how to laugh at stuff."

"I just show up ready for inspection. So you ain't been back here since . . . ?"

"No, not even. I never left New Hampshire."

"Wait a minute . . . You did the whole eight years up there in Portsmouth?"

"Sure did. Every day of it."

"Jesus. And then you got out?"

"Well, yeah. They had to let me out."

"And you went where?"

"Nowhere. Had nowhere to go. My mom died while I was on the inside, so there was nobody to go to. I just stayed in Portsmouth."

"Jesus."

"Like you stayed in Norfolk."

"Yeah, well, I guess."

"Sometimes people stay where they are. What's the point of going somewheres else?"

"Yeah, that's what happens sometimes, but to stay in the town where your prison is, you'd think . . ."

"It's not that bad a town. It's a pretty bad prison, but the town's okay."

"Jesus, kid . . . Hey?"

"What?"

"Listen, how the hell did you find me?"

"Internet. You can find anybody on the Internet."

"That's fucked."

"No, it's nice."

"So whaddaya do in Portsmouth?"

"I'm a stocking clerk, at the Navy PX."

* * *

Asleep on the pool table, Meadows's right heel blocks any shot at the corner pocket. Billy is stretched out in a booth, his cheek stuck to the leatherette, his open mouth feeling like a Hoover bag. In his dream he has been desperate to take a leak, but the urinal is upside down and the commode is overflowing and the ladies' room has disappeared entirely. He has to go somewhere, desperately, so he pisses skyward, at the TV set, *Cops*, which explodes on contact with his forceful stream, waking him up. He groans. He tries to work up some saliva. The shoulder hurts, the hips hurt, the back hurts. This morning even his ear lobes hurt. He struggles to get out of the booth. An open pizza box sits on the table.

Well into their drunk, Meadows said he was hungry and asked about the grille part of Billy B's Bar 'n Grille. There used to be a grille. Billy told him he used to put out a damn good burger, with a nice slice of raw onion and nothing else, except for mustard or ketchup, of course. No lettuce or pickles or crap. But over time his customers, young sailors back then, lost interest in honest hamburgers, so he let the grille go to rust. To feed

Meadows he ordered out some pizza and by the time it arrived he sent O'Toole home and closed the place down. He and the boy he once took to prison got down to some serious drinking and pizza eating and pool shooting and burying the past.

Billy makes his way to the urinal and sweet relief. The forceful stream flows only in his dreams. It takes so long these days. Finished, he washes his hands and throws some cold water on his face. He dries his hands in his short hair.

There is one piece of pizza left in the box, and he eats it cold as he draws two short beers. He calls out, "Now, reveille, reveille, drop your cocks and grab your socks! All hands turn to, prepare to relieve the watch, reveille!"

It's silly, he knows, but he gets a kick out of it anyway.

"Reveille, reveille, reveille! All those desiring to do so, lay down to the do-so locker and do so."

It doesn't work on Meadows. Billy has to stir the kid, push him around a little bit. Finally, he wakes up and takes the short beer Billy offers him.

"I'm still fucked up a little from last night," Billy says. "I'm getting too old for this shit, frankly. Sometimes I think I've had my share and should quit drinkin' altogether."

He says this and drinks the beer.

Meadows gets off the pool table and makes his uncertain way to the men's room. Billy wipes down the bar and empties the ashtrays. When Meadows comes out of the head, Billy says, "I love it, you know. It's priceless."

"What's that?"

"The U-S-N. They put you in the brig, put the big cock to you, a DD for rippin' off the PX, and then eight years later they hire you to work in another PX."

"I got five people under me."

"How'd that happen?"

"I worked hard. Did my job. I learned that from you."

"Jesus. No, I mean, how'd you get the job in the first place?"

"A brig sergeant helped me, after I got out."

"Fuck me. I was sure those jarheads'd kill you in there."

"I thought so too, in the beginning. It was kinda hard. But then they all go off to new duty and you're still there and the new guys just don't want any problem from you."

"You? You never made a problem for nobody."

"Tried not to. I got along just fine, after the first few years."

"You steal anything?"

"Yeah, but then I guess I grew out of that. There wasn't much to steal in there. After I got out, I never had the urge."

Billy laughs. Even that hurts. "Well, I'm pleased to hear that, 'cause next time somebody else gets to take you to the brig. This chaser is done chasin'."

"Listen, Billy, there's something been bothering me."

"Shoot."

"I'm sorry I ran, at the end."

"That's been bothering you?"

"Yeah."

"For all these years?"

"Yeah."

"Get over it. You didn't get far. Listen up, I'm sorry I worked you over."

"That's all right. What else could you do?"

"You wanna get some breakfast or somethin'? There's Mexicans in No'fuck now, we could get some chorizo con huevos. You got the balls for it, we qualify for menudo. Whaddaya say?"

"There is something I would like to do, if you're up for it. You got a car?"

"Do I have a car? I'm a businessman. Of course, I got a car."

* * *

It is not much of a car. A twenty-year-old Ford Taurus purchased at a good price from a customer whose bar tab had reached the point of becoming a serious debt. The tires are bald, the radio doesn't work, and the interior smells a bit fecal. Billy is a good driver, though, in spite of his hangover. At times he does drive dangerously fast. It doesn't bother Meadows—the grace of having nothing left to lose—but the instinct to survive is strong.

"Railroad crossing, Billy."

Billy slows down, looks for the crossing. There is none.

A light drizzle starts. The wiper blades have bad spots and rub wrong, making an unpleasant noise. They are driving through rural Virginia.

"You know what amazes me about you?" says Meadows.

"Could be anything. I'm an amazing dude."

"That you would lock up your bar, get in your car, and drive me you don't know where."

"I didn't think it would take so fuckin' long."

"We're almost there."

Meadows has been referring to a folded sheet of paper, on which a map has been reproduced. From the Internet, he explains to Billy.

"So where we at?" asks Billy, giving in at last to some curiosity. "It's pretty much boondocks out here."

"It's Sunday morning and we're going to church."

"No fuckin' way. Out in the boonies to go to church? I gotta tell you, kid, I ain't a big fan of church no matter where it is. Church is like Schwarzenegger movies: you seen one, you seen them all. If it was just boring that'd be one thing. Lots of stuff is boring, you live with it. But church has hurt more people than it's helped. *Killed* more. I'd hate to be God and have all that on my conscience. Allah is great. Show me. The whole deal right from the get-go was cooked up by some dudes wantin' to control other dudes. This is it, buddy, there ain't no more. Don't buy any pie in the sky."

"You don't think there's a heaven?"

"Can't quite picture it. Like, what do you *do* there?"

"You don't have to do anything. That's the whole idea. That's what makes it heaven. All the stuff you had to do is down here."

"The angels must be at each other's throats, outa sheer boredom. Now, you know all those angels doin' nothin' has gotta lead to mischief."

"Maybe you can't understand it. I don't mean you, I mean anybody. You can't imagine it, nobody can. I can't. But that don't mean it don't exist. It's got to."

"The odds are long against it, lad, and even if there is such a place, I'll bet you there's no rules about who gets in. *Everybody* gets in. And church has nothin' to do with it."

"This church, though, you're gonna like this church. You're gonna *love* it."

"I don't think so. Happy to give you a ride, but if it's all the same to you, I'll stay in the car, catch forty winks."

"Give it five minutes. If you aren't tickled pink we'll leave."

"Tickled pink? In church?"

"You'll see."

"Don't tell me you found Jesus up there in prison. Must be He spends a lot of time in prison, 'cause that's where everybody seems to find Him."

"I found Jesus in the two guys who took me there."

"Whoa."

"That's the truth. Two strangers risked their careers and a lot more just to show compassion to a messed-up kid—"

"Whoa, whoa, whoa—"

"That's Jesus to me."

"It wasn't like that. It was just—"

"I know what it was. I was there. And I'm long overdue saying thanks for that."

"Thanks? How the hell can you thank me for what I did to you? You should be cursin' me up one side and down the other. You should be kickin' my ass. Listen up, if I had any real compassion, I would have took you all the way to the border and let you slip into Canada."

"I wouldn't have gone."

"I shoulda made you."

"I wouldn't have known how."

"I shoulda showed you."

Two

It is a humble church for simple people who get up on a Sunday morning and put on their best clothes and go there. It might have been a barn once, and the parsonage the farm house. Maybe the people who lived and worked on the farm died and their children did not want to be farmers, or the land proved more valuable than the farm. For whatever reason the farm is no more. Small houses dot what would have been fields of beans. The church lacks a steeple and stained glass, but it makes up for all that with spirit.

Billy and Meadows enter into a congregation already on its feet, shouting out, keeping up with and sometimes getting ahead of the eight-piece choir in red and white robes. A big-rumped woman hammers on a piano.

The entrance of two white men, unshaven and smelling of stale smoke and beer, draws some notice, but that is momentary. Pew space is made for the strangers, and they stand awkwardly, no spirit moving them likewise.

To Billy's relief, the hymn ends and they are able to sit down. He checks his Timex. Three minutes, more or less, to go.

The preacher takes the pulpit. He is white-haired and moves with the aid of two canes. He casts a priestly gaze at the two visitors, then lifts his head to the congregation at large and says, "Jesus and Judas were *friends*."

Billy leans toward Meadows and whispers, "Oh, my fucking God. Is that who I think it is?"

Meadows smiles and nods. "I told you you'd like this."

Mule!

Billy is convinced that the sermon is extemporized, the planned sermon thrown out at the last moment, once Mule realized who was in his church. The lesson of the day had to turn to the danger of evil companions.

Billy is wildly amused. He turns and looks around at the others. He wants to tell them.

"Oh, a good man can be laid low by a mean friend, a so-called friend . . ." An amen is laid on that, and Billy himself seconds it.

"A *preacher?*" Billy whispers to Meadows. "Mule's a *preacher?* That dude was a first-class gambler, drinker, and cocksman."

Meadows goes, "Shhhh . . ."

"And a bunch of other shit, you can be sure. How the hell did you find this church?"

The Internet, of course.

"Oh, yes, in the spirit of friendship, have a drink . . . have a toke . . . have a snort. The devil has a friendly face and a winning way. But behind that smile . . . as behind the kiss of Judas . . ."

Billy flatters himself that Mule's sermon is ironic and for his own benefit. In truth, the Reverend Mulhall sees them only for what they are: two white wandering and wayward drunks working off a hangover. In the house of God all manner of men are welcome. He does not recognize them, though as he preaches, somewhere deep in his memory the tiniest tinkle is heard and feared.

He finishes his sermon and an echoing of "Amens" rolls wall to wall, Billy's among them.

"I see we have some visitors this morning. Welcome to our church and Sunday service. Would you like to stand and introduce yourselves?"

Billy doesn't need to be asked twice. He is up and at a kind of shaky attention. He snaps off a salute, which hurts his shoulder and makes him momentarily cringe. Then he sounds off, "William J. Buddusky, Signalman First Class, US Navy, retired."

The Reverend Mulhall fairly totters at the pulpit. He has to hold on to its sides. Billy smiles and adds, "The original Billy Bad-Ass."

Heads turn to each other and whisper, so that a hum, a buzz fills the church. Meadows tugs at Billy's sleeve, but Billy pulls him in the other direction instead, up to his feet, saying, "And guess who this lad is?"

The Reverend Mulhall by now knows who it is and realizes his past is revisiting him, but he is saved from any further response when the church doors fly open and Clarence Taylor bursts inside.

A casual glance at the congregation would confirm that the women here outnumber the men. Most of the husbands are missing, men who send their wives to church alone. Everyone knows why: to see the first football game of the day in solitude. Clarence Taylor is one of those husbands. His appearance in church is usually occasioned by an event with no excuses: a wedding, a funeral, a baptism, but now here he is, on his own, shivering in his undershirt, a wiry, excited man of fifty. He runs down the aisle throwing up his arms and fairly screaming, "They got him! They got him!"

The Reverend raises his hand for calm and says, "Who got who, Clarence?"

"That sumbitch Saddam! The army got Saddam Hussein! In a spider hole!"

Mrs. Taylor is mortified to have her husband cussing in church.

* * *

The remainder of the service is truncated and hurried so that everyone can rush home and see for themselves, for the first of innumerable times, the ravaged despot say, "Ahhhh," and submit to the bald medic's latexed fingers probing his filthy matted hair for elite Republican Guards of lice.

The post-service niceties are foregone and the congregation is scattered in seconds.

The drizzle has stopped, though clouds threaten more rain. Left at the entrance to the church are Reverend Mulhall, his wife—a plump woman with the Biblical name Ruth—and the old sailor and his prisoner.

"I thought you were dead," Mule says to Billy.

Billy shrugs and says, "Hell, I might be. I mean, how does anyone know?"

Ruth possesses a naturally generous spirit and a womanly way of salvaging awkward social situations. She invites the two visitors to Sunday dinner.

It is ham! In a Coca-Cola sauce, with yams and lima beans.

While Ruth puts the finishing touches on the meal, the two old salts and their charge watch the news coverage. It is a good distraction.

The Butcher of Baghdad, the most feared among a fearsome breed, now a derelict and nothing more than ridiculous.

"How the mighty fall," observes Mule, in keeping with his theology.

Billy finds it hard to believe that he and Saddam are about the same age. He is put off by the man's cowardice.

Mule goes on in wonder, "Within sight of his palace . . . *one* of his many palaces . . . living in a hole in the ground. On this, his worst day, he has $750,000 in his pocket, and only God knows how much in Switzerland, in France. . . . Now, just the rags on his back. Nothing to negotiate."

Billy says, "The dude's a punk. Everybody else is supposed to fight to the death. If it was reversed, our guy'd be the same way, hidin' in some hole."

"You don't know that," says Mule.

"The risk always goes to somebody else. The sacrifice is always somebody else's, and somebody else's child."

"I'm trying to listen to this."

What's to hear? The first of legions of pundits, predicting with great expertise that Saddam's capture will either increase the attacks on Coalition Forces or decrease them. Some coalition.

"This is it, don't you think? This has got to be the end . . . or the beginning of the end, right?" asks Meadows, with an odd and obvious anxiety.

Billy finds himself watching Meadows more than Hussein, because for today at least the monster is on an endless loop: open wide, where's those lice? He tunes out Mule, who has next Sunday's sermon already in the works, trying it out in the rough on a smaller crowd. But Meadows has a sunk-down-deep look that Billy remembers from before, borne of hopelessness, fear, and irony, not unlike, really, the mien of old Saddam.

"I wouldn't bet on it meaning much of anything," Billy says.

After a moment, Meadows says, "It's a great thing they got this guy. It's good that nobody in Iraq has to worry about what he's gonna do to them . . . but I can't help wondering . . . if last week, or last year, our president would have given up his daughter's life for it."

* * *

Billy vaguely remembers his last home-cooked meal. Gloria had an attack of domesticity and made him Swiss steak. It was disgusting.

His arms corral the plate and he goes at his food with great enthusiasm.

"Home cookin'," he sighs. "More than I ever bargained for, wham-bam, thank you, ma'am."

"You don't have a wife?" asks Ruth.

"No, ma'am. I do have a lady friend, but she don't cook. She has other talents, if you know what I mean."

"And you, Mr. Meadows, are you single or married?"

"Oh, I married a wonderful woman, Mrs. Mulhall."

"That's a blessing."

"Yes, it is. A good woman makes all the difference in a man's life," Mule adds.

"She was a special needs person," says Meadows.

"If she married you, kid, she had to have special needs," cracks Billy.

"She was developmentally disabled."

"Retarded, you mean," says Billy.

"Just kind of borderline, a little slow, but she had a heart as big as . . . anything. And she was a real pretty girl. With a great big smile and the whitest teeth. I lost her last January, cancer of the breast."

Billy stops eating.

"Sorry, kid, but you know me. I got a smart mouth."

"We pay for the things we say," says Mule.

"Put it on my tab, kid."

"And the things we do, we pay for it all eventually, sooner or later, just like old Saddam Hussein."

Mule has been restraining himself, out of respect for his wife. She knows what transpired back then, but he doesn't want to expose her to any more of it, even from this distant point. He needs more time, anyway, to process his feelings. So much has happened just this morning, in the world and in this house. For over thirty years he has lived with the responsibility for a man's death, and now he finds the man is alive, that heavy penance has been lifted from his shoulders, praise Jesus. A sense of soaring freedom lifts him from the anchors of his two canes. Now he can run, he can fly. On the other hand . . . he paid dearly for that prank, which now turns out to be only as harmless as he had originally intended. Nine months behind bars of a three-year sentence, grim and humiliating confinement, loss of pension, a Bad Conduct Discharge. Can he now petition the Navy for a full pardon and restoration of benefits? Well, of course he can petition the Navy for anything he wants to, but the Navy does not have to listen, and his court-martial was not for murder or even for manslaughter but for a host of other infractions: AWOL, destruction of government property, assault on a Shore Patrol, for all of which he was guilty, but so was Billy. Everything considered, though, he is grateful to God for it, because in that misery he found his true calling and gathered 'round him all the joys a man can possibly desire. Just one more thing, Lord, I beseech You: keep me from wringing Billy's neck.

"Do you have children?" Ruth asks Meadows.

Meadows hesitates. "We had just the one, a son."

"Richard and I have a boy and a girl, and we have four grandchildren."

"Richard?" says Billy. "That's your name?"

"You don't even know each other's first names?" asks Ruth.

"It never came up. Old Dick never told us his name, did you, Dickie?"

"All right, it's only a name."

"I don't think I ever met a brother named Richard . . . or Dick," says Billy.

"Richard Pryor," Mule reminds him. "Dick Gregory."

"You're right!"

"You just never noticed."

"Is it a comedian thing? Because you used to be funny."

"Honey, don't you have some coffee and pie for these men, before we send them on their way?" says Mule, eager to put an end to the Dick business. In the Navy no one ever uses first names. They are essentially unknown. With the obvious exception of Billy Bad-Ass.

"I have peach cobbler for dessert," says Ruth.

"Oh, man, this is livin'!" says Billy. "Peach cobbler!" He opens his cigar case, concealing the three joints he has hidden in there, and offers, "Cigar?"

In the kitchen, Ruth takes her time with the coffee and cobbler, listening in on what happens next.

"No," says her husband, "and I'd like you not to have one either. We don't allow smoking in our house. You can go out on the porch if you want to smoke."

"So you don't smoke anymore either, huh?"

"No, I do not."

"Don't suppose you'd have any hard liquor anywhere."

"No, I wouldn't."

"Because the kid and I got so shitface last night we could use the hair of the dog."

"I'm good," says Meadows. "That great meal fixed me up fine. And your sermon, Mule . . . I had no idea you could talk so good."

"Meadows," says Mule, "I'm glad you prevailed over your hardships."

"Well . . . if I have. Doing the best I can."

"You seem to have turned out a decent man."

"Try to be."

"I regret I played a role in what happened back then."

Billy shakes his head, as though trying to defog his brain. "What the hell did you do to the old Mule, preacher? Where're you keepin' him?"

"I grew up, Billy, and I grew old. Thank God I found a purpose along the way."

"You don't have to feel sorry," says Meadows. "You did what you had to do."

"Well told," says Billy. "The Old Man tells the MAA, the MAA tells you, and you go do it. The kid knows that much."

"I'm just curious, Billy. How much time did you have to do?"

"Time? Where?"

"Brig time. How much brig time did you have to pull?"

"I never did a day of brig time, man. Came close a couple times but—"

"You weren't court-martialed?"

"Me? Hell, no. For what? All I got was a plate in my head and a hundred percent disability and a fare-thee-well, don't let the hatch hit you on the ass on your way out."

"Wait a minute, you got disability?"

"Fuckin' A. I'm disabled, like Meadows' old lady, may she rest in peace. It's not enough to live on, but it let me buy my own bar."

Mule is all but out of his seat, going for Billy's throat, before realizing he can't get up without his canes. He reaches down to the floor for a cane but is too impatient to use it for leverage. Instead, he swings it at Billy's head. Billy's reactions are still good enough to pull back out of range.

"Whoa!" he says.

Mule rants about the price he had to pay while Billy was enjoying his disability payments, and an honorable discharge.

"Calm down, old timer, you'll bust a blood vessel."

Meadows is at a loss to explain Mule's outburst. He tries to rein them in and get some clarity. He's disappointed to know that nothing was as he had imagined it, over all the years, beginning on the day he was delivered to the Marine brig in Portsmouth, New Hampshire.

Wrath is one of the Seven Deadly Sins, and Mule regards it as the most easily avoided. He calms his inner pull to anger and explains to Meadows that after they dropped him at the prison they went on what they thought would be their separate ways back to their common destination, the transient barracks at Norfolk, and hopefully their new orders, possibly to Vietnam, a war whose loss of validity was approaching critical mass. That was the big bogus. The little one was the detail they had carried out as ordered.

Instead they went on a big-time wound-cleansing binge, the last time Mule ever tasted alcohol. Sick of, or embarrassed by, the sight of each other, they went AWOL together alone on opposite sides of the street, after disposing of their Navy issue sidearms in a US Mail collection box.

When finally collared by the Shore Patrol, they were gently chided and pushed along toward the van. The two Shore Patrol were just sailors like them and were amused by their antics, scuttlebutt of which was already making its way through the system. That's when Mule came up with his impromptu practical joke. His whispered suggestion was that, at the count of three, they each take out a Shore Patrol and . . . well, there was no *and*.

"Now I remember!" Billy shouts, as though coming out of a long amnesia, which in fact, is pretty much the case. "We were wasted on Wild Turkey and beer, no sleep in a couple days, pissed-off mode. Old Mule says, 'You get your man, I'll get mine. Count of three.' I had no time to think about it before I hear *three*. Well, I whirl and bring one up from the ground. *Pow!* That second-class bosun went into the air and down for the count. I look over and Mule is pissin' his pants laughin' at me, and, ship-mate, that's the lastest thing I remember, and till now I didn't even remember that much. Woke up five days later in sick bay. Fractured skull, heebie-jeebies. They patched me up, dried me out, filled me full of that good hospital chow, and before I could say, 'Aye-aye, sir,' they had me out of the Navy."

"They said you were dead. They popped me and dragged us both to the van. I was near unconscious. The driver of the van checked you out and said you were dead."

"Sorry to disappoint you. Takes more than a pussy Shore Patrol to cash my check."

"I've been living with that for over thirty years."

"I forgive you."

"Fuck you," says Mule.

Their heads turn to the sound of a coffee cup breaking on the kitchen floor.

* * *

The cobbler is crusty on top and sweet and moist inside, like so many Norfolk bar girls of Billy's memory. The coffee has chicory, an exotic addition far better than broken eggshells. Good food promotes good feelings, and when what's done is done, it should always be followed by cobbler and a bit of Christian forgiveness.

"A grand plan designed by geniuses to be run by idiots," says Mule, defining the US Navy.

"I've heard that said," says Meadows. "A lot."

"And the idiots were givin' all the orders, to *us*, so what did that make us?"

"Pawns of idiots."

"What I think happened is," says Billy, "they looked at my outstanding record of service—"

Mule snorts.

"No, it's true. I was four-point-oh, A. J. Squaredaway. Okay, on the shy side of insubordination half the time, but I could get away with that because of my dashing good looks and my boyish charm."

Mule snorts a second time.

"Getting mixed up with you two was the only black mark on my record, excuse the expression. So what I think happened was, the Navy got rattled when they saw they damned near killed me—"

"Self-defense."

"No, no, overreaction, man."

"You're talking about *now*. Back then nobody cared about overreaction."

"They *disabled* me, man. They could of had a veggie on their hands, so it was in the Navy's best interests to cut me loose and keep me happy."

"Were you happy?" asks Meadows.

"That's another story."

"And me?" asks Mule. "Why'd they come down so hard on me?"

"Well, they had to put the cock to somebody, that's how it works. Some bad shit went down, somebody's got to bleed for it."

"The black man."

"Here we go. It's always the black thing. Always was. You know, not everything that happens is about being black or white."

"It is if you're black and in America."

"All right, if it makes you feel better."

"All of this happened so long ago," says Ruth, who has been nothing if not a calming influence. "Isn't it best to put it behind you? Enjoy the lives you have now?"

"Words of wisdom, ma'am, words of wisdom. And outstanding cobbler."

"I couldn't figure out the Navy while I was in it," says Mule, "no sense in trying to figure it out now."

Billy goes, "Yo," to Mule, in a whisper, and nods toward Meadows. He sits on a cushioned wicker chair, arms on his knees, sinking fast inside. His body, overweight now, trembles. Except for the added bulk, he looks so much like the lost kid they saw that winter's morning in the office of the master-at-arms, waiting in handcuffs to be taken away.

Meadows must realize they're looking at him. He hasn't said anything in some time, and now no one is saying anything.

"I never had any friends," he says.

"Oh, that can't be true," says Ruth.

Mule reaches over and puts his hand on her knee, silencing her.

"I knew people—everybody knows people—people I work with and stuff, but I never had anybody go out of their way for me, take a risk for me, like you two did."

"It wasn't that far out of the way," says Billy. "Forget about it."

"Can't you see he's trying to say something?" says Mule.

"Yeah, I can see that, which is why I'm tryin' to give the dude an out before he gets all weepy."

"Don't worry about me, Billy, I'm all cried out."

Billy presses his fork against the last of the crumbs, lifts it to his mouth.

"Go ahead, Meadows," says Mule.

"I came here because of my son."

"Your son?" asks Ruth.

"A little less than a year ago he joined the Marines."

"He *what?*" says Billy, incredulous. The notion of one's own flesh and blood becoming a Marine was a family disappointment too deep for the old sailor to grasp.

"He joined the Marines . . . and now he's dead."

"Aw, shit, kid."

"He died a hero. In Baghdad, when his convoy was ambushed. He unloaded his weapon on them and died fighting with his bayonet in his hand."

"When did this happen?" asks Mule.

"What's today? Oh, it's Sunday, right. Church. He's coming home tonight. To Washington. They're going to bury him at Arlington, with full honors. I don't think I can face it alone. I need a friend. Two would be better."

* * *

Billy smokes a cigar out on the porch, sitting on the rail, shivering in the cold. He feels bad for Meadows, of course, but what can he do? What can anyone do that is real? He showed the kid a good drunk last night. That has to count for something. That was real.

Mule is all over the kid with sympathy and shit. Billy can hear some of it, and he answers it out there on the porch, talking to himself. He cuts the glowing end off his cigar and saves the rest. He goes back inside and sits on the piano stool, away from them, listening for as long as he can stand it to Mule's spiritual guidance and comfort, which the kid seems to be lapping up. He wonders if Meadows is just being polite, listening to Mule's bullshit. He's the politest kid Billy ever ran into.

To be honest, Billy is not unimpressed with Mule's acumen. The dude seems to know his stuff. Probably he *does* help some of those people in his church. When he gives Meadows the guarantee, however, *promises* him that someday he will join his son and his wife in a better place, well, that tears it for Billy.

"What better place? Las Vegas? Miami Beach?"

"He knows the place I speak of."

"Where's this place on the map, show it to him. The kid's got a map in the car. Tell him what it looks like. Maybe he can find it on the Internet."

"Only when you see it will you know it, and in your case, signalman, it's odds-on you'll never see it."

"Then I guess I won't miss it."

"Oh, you will miss it dearly, every moment of eternity. Do you know how long eternity is, Billy?"

"No, but I guess I'm gonna hear about it right now."

"If a sparrow picked up a grain of earth and flew to the moon at his usual speed, then dropped the grain and flew back again for another speck, and flew back to the moon . . . by the time that sparrow moved all of Earth to the moon, eternity would have just begun."

Ruth smiles. She has heard this lesson before, and often enough to give that little sparrow a pretty good start.

"Tell me this, padre. Out of all the billions of people hanging out in your heaven, don't you think maybe one of 'em could have got word back to the rest of us?"

"One of them did."

"Weak on the details. If you ask me."

"I'm not asking you."

"It's two pounds of shit packed into a one-pound bag. Excuse my French, missus—or whaddaya say now, excuse my *freedom*. One day you are, and the next day you ain't anymore. Now you exist, now you don't. Heaven is just another promise made by people who can't keep a promise, to keep other people in line. But if they only knew there wasn't no heaven, they'd have to make more of what they had here, and that might make this a much better world. I'm sorry for your loss, kid, but I ain't gonna blow smoke up your ass. The worst thing in the world has landed on you and now you got to deal with it."

Mule says, "You were a menace when you were young and now that you're old you're just a fool."

"I got your fool danglin', fool."

"Okay, okay, okay," Meadows interjects. "I never meant to cause trouble. Please—"

"No problem, kid. I'll take you to bury your boy. I may not get you into heaven, but, goddammit, I can get you to Arlington."

He stands up and sticks the remains of his unlit cigar between his teeth and bites down. "We'd better get goin'."

"Mule . . . please? It would mean a lot to me."

Mule looks for the best way to say no.

"We're getting close to Christmas. It's my busy time," says Mule.

"Mine too," says Billy, "but things come up, don't they? That's life."

"You're employed?"

"I told you, I own a bar. I'm *self*-employed. Let's go, kid. Don't you worry, though, old Mule'll pray for you."

"Indeed I will. As you can see, Meadows, I don't get around that well these days."

"It's just in the car," says Meadows.

"Richard, could I see you in the kitchen for a moment please?"

Mule pushes himself up with his canes and follows his wife to the kitchen.

When they are out of the room, Billy says with a smile, "He's comin' with."

"You think so? He said—"

"Don't matter what he said. His old lady's gonna make him."

Billy is right in this, though wrong in his reasoning why.

"You're a heartbreaker, kid. She can't resist you. She's in the kitchen right now, sayin', 'You got to go with that poor boy. He needs you.'"

Incredibly, that is exactly what she is saying, and exactly at that moment.

Mule, on the other hand, is saying, "They've got plenty of chaplains there. He will have qualified people to counsel him."

"Maybe so," says his wife, "but he is going to need someone to protect him from that Billy Bad-Ass person."

Mule chuckles. "Well, I do know from personal experience that things can go sideways when that man is around, but that was back in the day, back when there was an overriding authority, when he was outranked by assholes and had to take their orders."

"What in the world has happened to your vocabulary?"

"I'm sorry, dear."

"That young man has lost his son. We can only imagine what that must be like. He's in a very vulnerable state, and that other one is, well, coarse. To put the two of them together, alone, at this moment, is a recipe for disaster."

"Billy has his faults, Lord knows, but I must admit that his heart is usually in the right place."

"Will his heart guide him? Because I think he's rudderless. You have to do this, Richard. You have to go with them. I'll pack you an overnight bag."

Three

"You have to wear that collar wherever you go?" Billy asks.

Mule sits in the backseat of the Taurus.

"I choose to wear it," he says.

"Proud of it, are you?"

"Pride is a sin. It's who I am now."

"Like we wore our chevrons and our hash marks, remember? I know dudes even wore 'em on their skivvies."

"That was pride, some kind of pride, I don't know what."

"Was it a sin?"

"No, it was just stupid."

"You were proud of your chevrons."

"I was stupid too."

"Why don't you take it off and relax," says Billy.

"I am relaxed," says Mule

The bag his wife packed for him is at his feet. She's also given him a bottle of water to carry, and he sips from it. Good hydration has become a duty of age.

They've passed through Richmond and it is night, on the northbound interstate. Billy has slowed down. He drives the speed limit, at times five or ten miles below the speed limit. Mule worries he might have some trouble with night vision, as he does himself.

"I notice you don't wear glasses, Billy."

"Funniest thing . . . I used to, but last year my eyes turned around on me. I'm back to where I was. I still need them to read, but I can drive and watch TV and if I ever went to a movie again I wouldn't need them."

"What about at night?"

"I'm mostly inside at night, at the bar."

At a rest stop, Billy pulls off. He promises them—warns them, really—that this will be their last stop before DC. He's been stopping about every forty-five minutes, so it's likely there will be still one more.

They walk the path to the men's room. Meadows stays with Mule, who is slower, while Billy hustles on ahead of them.

"Thanks for coming, Mule. Can I still call you Mule?"

"You can call me whatever you want to. I owe you, son."

"I wish you wouldn't say that. You don't owe me anything. I owe you. You could of given me the bum's rush, you didn't have to do the things you did."

"And we shouldn't have. No, sir, we shouldn't have, but what a sad sight you were. Not to mention what a miscarriage of justice. No point in digging it up again. What's gone is gone."

"But is it, ever?"

Billy is still at one of the two aluminum urinals when they get there. Meadows offers Mule the other slot. The Reverend steps forward, hooking his two canes over his left wrist as he undoes his fly.

Billy chuckles. "Where was it we got in that shithouse brawl? Richmond? DC?"

"New York. Port Authority."

"Was it there?"

"I think it was," says Meadows.

Billy laughs, remembering.

"I remember," says Meadows, "how satisfying it felt then to hit a man. I'm a little ashamed now to admit it, but it did. That was the last time I ever hit another person. I never even spanked Larry Junior. I didn't have to, really. He was always a good boy."

"You did eight years in the brig and never was in a fight?" asks Billy.

"I didn't say I was never in a fight. I said I never hit a man again after that brawl in the Port Authority. I got the shit kicked out of me once in the brig."

"And you didn't fight back?"

"No point. There was five of them."

"That's the point at which there *is* a point."

"What happened?" asks Mule.

"My mom had sent me a carton of cigarettes and they wanted them. Funny thing is, I'd already stopped smoking by that time."

"So why didn't you just give them the cigarettes?"

"They were from my mother."

Billy finally finishes. Meadows steps up to take his place.

"I know it was with some Marines," Billy remembers. "The brawl. *Our* brawl. What was the beef?"

"I don't think there ever was one," says Meadows.

"You called one of them a dickhead," says Mule.

"Doesn't sound like me."

"No, what he said," says Meadows, "was the Marine didn't have to undo thirteen buttons like we did, to take a leak, all a Marine had to do was take off his hat."

Billy laughs again.

"Does that sound like you?"

"A little."

"We were lucky we wasn't arrested," says Meadows.

"As I recall, you already was," says Billy.

"And the rest of us soon would be," says Mule.

They wash their hands at the sink. Billy is holding his under the hot air dryer.

A teamster comes in and takes a urinal. He shows the broad beam, the big gut, the dissipation of twenty years of junk food and sitting endless hours in the cab of a sixteen-wheeler.

"Hey, mister? You in one of those big rigs out there?" Billy asks.

"Yeah," the truck driver answers flatly. He is weary from the road.

"What's the action like in those truck stop parking lots?"

"Excuse me?" The driver is about forty, but it's been a hard forty. He's taken enough shit, generally, to last a lifetime. He turns to Billy and zips up. "What's on your mind, old man?"

"How particular are you dudes about who sucks your cock?"

"Sir," says Mule, "I apologize for our friend. You don't deserve this abuse. Billy, help me back to the car."

Meadows is all but breathless, in a half-exciting, half-terrifying sense of déjà vu.

"Old man, you ought to watch what you say to strangers," says the truck driver.

"Because I heard," Billy says, undaunted, "that a teamster'll pay five for a whore, ten for a dude, and twenty for a dog."

"Okay, stop it! Right now!" Mule insists. "Meadows, take him to the car."

Meadows grabs Billy's arm and tugs him away. Billy is laughing. Mule stays behind to try to make some reasonable explanation to the offended party, though none comes quickly to mind. What he says is, "This is a man who when he feels most powerless has to find an enemy. It was your misfortune to be close at hand."

"Powerless? About what?"

"Things pile up as you get old."

"Well, it's a great way to lose what teeth he got left."

"Yes, it is, and he would think it worth the loss. Again, sir, I'm sorry."

"Yeah. All right."

* * *

Back on the interstate it starts to rain. Billy slows down to 55, leans slightly forward. He struggles to see past the hypnotic wipers.

Mule has been scolding him, to unknown effect since Billy does not respond to his admonitions. Every so often, he believes, you have to roil up the air or it takes on a heaviness that is suffocating.

The car suddenly fills with light. A semi is tailgating them.

"It's the fuckin' teamster," says Billy. "All right, fucker, you want to play, I'll play."

He punches the accelerator. The little Taurus speeds to 65 . . . 75 . . . but the semi stays right on his tail.

"Pull off the road!" yells Mule. "You can't outrun him."

"Hold on! I'm gonna hit the brakes and jackknife the fucker!"

"No!" yells Meadow. "My son! I have to be there."

"You'll kill us all, you son of a bitch!" yells Mule.

Billy slows down, rolls down the window, and holds his middle finger aloft. Rain flies into the car.

The big truck passes them and cuts in front of them dangerously close, creating a deluge against the windshield. Billy slows down to almost a stop, laughing.

Mule realizes that Billy has been back in his life for just a few hours and he has already used two ripping profanities and one crudity.

As though reading his mind, Billy says, "Padre, you're gonna hafta either tighten up your mouth or loosen up your collar."

"I will do my best to control my mouth," says Mule.

The collar stays on.

* * *

They find Arlington National Cemetery easily enough, but what is supposed to happen there on a drizzling Sunday night in December? Surely not a funeral. Neither Billy nor Mule have thought to question Meadows about the particulars. The important thing seemed to be to bring the father to the son, which they thought they were doing.

"Where are we supposed to go, kid?" asks Billy.

Meadows has a pouch full of Internet maps and other papers. He shuffles through the mess.

"Dover Air Force Base."

"That's in Delaware."

"Right. Dover, Delaware."

"So what are we doing here?"

"I don't know."

"You said Arlington."

"That's what they said."

"But now you're saying Dover."

"First Dover. They got to fly in somewhere, so they fly in to Dover. Doves fly . . . doves maybe sometimes fly in to Dover."

Billy tries not to lose patience. He's got an unhinged person here, like the last time. It's all right to indulge him. And it's not like Billy has anything better to do in Norfolk. O'Toole is capable of running the bar, even drunk, as long as he's not too drunk, and even then, what's the worst that can happen. The cops close him down . . . the place burns to the ground . . . so what?

"All right, kid, it's Dover, where the doves come back to roost. I'm guessing in there you got a map to Dover."

"Looks like about an hour 'n' a half. You want me to drive?"

"Can you?"

"I'm fifty-two years old."

"Mule is sixty-six if he's a day, but I wouldn't let him drive."

Billy is relieved to turn over the wheel. He gets into the back seat with Mule.

"Go sit up front," Mule tells him.

"Naw, we'll sit back here and pretend we're big shots."

As the car heads toward Annapolis, Billy sinks back and says, "Mule, my man, are you still able to give your wife a good fuck on a Saturday night?"

"What kind of question is that?" says Meadows. "You're a little out of line, Billy, if you don't mind my telling you."

"What? I'm curious."

Mule gives Billy an icy look.

"At our age it's a reasonable question. Of course, now, maybe she hates the idea . . . or maybe she could be just tired of the whole thing, like women get. They get tired of it long before we do. I don't know why, it's not like they have to do a whole lot besides just show up and lie down. We're the ones got to rock 'n' roll, if you know what I mean. We're the ones got to transform the parts, if you know what I mean, mister."

"Everyone always knows what you mean, Billy," says Mule.

"You make that sound like a bad thing."

"I don't talk about my sex life, with you or anyone. Decent people don't. It's called privacy. It's called respect for your wife, but you wouldn't know about that."

"Hold on. I respect your wife. Of course I do. But we're on a road trip here and I only wanted to know if you can still cut the mustard. Just makin' conversation on how the years have treated you."

He gets nowhere with Mule, who if he's not looking outside just closes his eyes.

"Now, Meadows, he's still a young man, in the prime of his life, you don't have to ask. He don't need Viagra to fly the flag. Do you, kid, need Viagra?"

"I haven't had sex in two years."

"Why not?"

"My wife was sick and then she died."

"Weren't you listening?" Mule admonishes.

"Well, yeah, but life goes on. Don't it? How long do you have to wait before . . . you know?"

"Longer than this," says Meadows. "I wouldn't know how to be with another girl. I wouldn't feel right."

"How're you supposed to feel?"

"Good. Like it's right."

"Definitely. I always feel that way."

"The young man is on a higher plane than you, when it comes to loving a woman," says Mule.

"Remember your first time?" Billy asks.

"No," says Meadows quickly.

"Everyone remembers his first time."

"I don't."

"Well, I do. I bought it for you."

"I told Mary about that. I fessed up to everything."

"I doubt it, you wouldn't tell her everything," says Billy, smiling. "Some of that you had the good sense you didn't want her to know. Fact is, she shouldn't of known any of it. Wasn't none of her business."

"I wanted no secrets from her."

"Now that's just stupid."

"No, that's smart."

"So you told her how you popped off in the girl's hand and we had to pay a readmission fee." He laughs.

Meadows laughs a little too. "Your memory's better than I worried it would be."

"You were in luv-v-v-v-v. That little whore swept you off your feet. She was a darlin' little whore."

"Shameful," says Mule.

"Looking back, I wish Mary had been the first and not that whore in Boston."

"Was it in Boston? I thought it was New York."

"It was in Boston."

"It was never about you getting laid, lad," says Mule. "It was about Billy getting you laid."

"Duh?" grunts Billy.

"He had to show you a good time, and he only knew his way."

"As I recall, you were there too."

"Yes, I didn't know any more than you did what a good time was, back in those days."

"Oh, it ain't that complicated, and it hasn't changed since then. A little whorin', a little drinkin', a little fightin'. All things in moderation. We did it all, and I think it was worth doin', at the time. If there was any beef about it, it was me thinkin' it would make your brig time easier and Mule thinkin' it would make it harder. So which was it, kid? Was I right or was I wrong."

Meadows looks down the highway. "Didn't make it any harder."

"See?" says Billy.

". . . Didn't make it any easier. It was just time, and it was long."

"Well, nothin' we could do about that. Short of lettin' you run."

They fall silent and before long they cross the Severn River Bridge into Delaware.

They find the main gate to the Dover Air Force Base and stop at the guard shack. Meadows lowers his window and tries to tell the guard why they are here. The guard seems confused.

"When is this funeral?" he asks.

"I'm not sure, exactly," says Meadows. "They said he'd be home today . . . and then they'd bury him in Arlington National Cemetery . . . with full military honors . . . and a Silver Star."

"From Iraq, right?"

"That's right, Iraq. He was killed in a firefight in Iraq. He was ambushed on a patrol. He died a hero."

"Yes, sir."

Billy leans forward and says, "You got a phone in that shack, lad?"

"Yes, sir."

"Get on it. Find out where this man's son is and make it happen that we can see him. We'll wait."

"What's the man's name?"

"Meadows. Lawrence Meadows, Junior. USMC. Lance Corporal."

Having calls answered by a knowing person is never easy under any circumstances. On a wet Sunday night it becomes more difficult. The three in the car sit and wait and watch the guard on the phone.

"What's wrong, I wonder," says Meadows.

"Just routine," says Billy. "He's a guard at a gate. He don't know nothin'."

"I wonder if there'll be cameras 'n' stuff."

"Cameras?"

"TV. You know, like you see, the coffins comin' off the plane . . . the honor guard . . . all that."

"Oh, yeah, the off-loading ceremony. I ain't seen that lately. Mule, have you seen that lately?"

"Not lately," says Mule.

"I think they knocked that off. It was bad for homeland morale, They put a blackout on that stuff. They remember 'Nam."

"Now that you mention it," says Meadows, "I think I did read in the papers, no more pictures of bodies coming home."

"I read the papers," says Mule, "but I don't believe them any-more. Not much better than TV. The same five old white guys own the whole works."

"What you're thinkin' of was, like, after the *Cole* got blown up or one of those other bombings. Then it rallied the people. Now it just depresses them."

"I think you owe it to the boys," says Meadows, "and to the guys in their units, and to the families. It's a respect thing, to cover them coming home. What are they afraid of?"

"They don't want to take any chances people might feel the wrong way."

"Do you even want it to be on TV?" asks Mule.

"Sure. Larry deserves that. They all do. They're all heroes."

The guard finally comes out of his shack.

"Gentlemen, the lance corporal's body is in transit. The plane's not due until 0800 hours tomorrow. Come back then and you'll be able to wait for the plane in the hangar."

"In transit," says Billy, more to himself. "Somebody's always in transit, somewhere, even when you're dead."

* * *

The Howard Johnson's has one vacancy left. The clerk assures them it's roomy enough and comfortable for three.

"I had assumed I'd have my own room," says Mule, showing signs of tiredness.

"Don't get cranky," says Billy, "we'll have you tucked in before you know it."

Meadows has opened a brown envelope from his file. From it he counts out in cash the eighty-two dollars for the room. The envelope is stuffed with cash.

"Whoa," says Billy. "What's with the wad?"

"Everybody at the PX took up a collection when they heard. They bought me a plane ticket and then gave me money to see me through the trip. I tried to turn it down, but they wouldn't let me. I really did need it anyway."

"See? You got friends. Not just us."

"They felt bad," says Meadows. "They felt they had to do something."

"We can pay our share," says Mule.

"No, I can't ask you to do that. This is on me. On the nice people who work and shop at the PX. Navy people."

"How much you got in there, kid?"

"I don't know. They told me but I forgot."

The room has two beds, a king and a queen. Mule lays claim to the queen, lying down and stretching out with a sigh.

Billy opens the small reefer. Nothing inside. A small white microwave sits above it. In the bathroom, a coffee maker is attached to a wall.

"Anybody hungry?" asks Billy.

Meadows has sat down on one of the two chairs, at a small round table. Mule has his eyes closed, but Billy knows he is not asleep.

"Remember the last time we shared a room in Wash DC? Got shitface on beer and I taught you a little semaphore?"

"I kept it up. I practiced in the brig. Nothin' else to do."

"No, shit? You made yourself a signalman?"

"Just the semaphore."

"C'mon, show me."

"It's been years."

"You never forget. Let's see what you got."

Mule's eyes open now. He watches Meadows get to his feet and flash his hands through the alphabet.

"Fuck me," says Billy. "Did you see that, Mule?"

"I saw it. I'm impressed."

"Fuckin' A. Has it down cold."

"Yeah," says Meadows. "Useless, but I know it."

Years ago, perhaps, Billy would have been insulted to be told his primary skill was useless, but now he more or less has to agree.

"It was never about gettin' a good job. It was about *doin'* a good job. It was about a tradition."

"Whatever it was about," says Mule dryly, "it was about then, not now."

"Why's everything have to be about now?" Billy wonders aloud, but no one has an answer. "If you wanna talk about now, I'm a little hungry now. That ham lasted good, but it's time to take on more groceries."

"I could eat something," says Meadows. "But I want to stay by the phone."

"Why? Nobody knows we're here."

Which reminds Mule that he's forgotten to call Ruth. He gets up and dials through and tells her where they are. He gives her the number. He tells her he will call again tomorrow. He says, "Good night. I love you too."

Billy feels a pang of envy.

"Don't neither of you dudes have a wireless phone?" Billy asks.

"Never had the need," says Meadows.

"What about you, padre? Don't you have to be on call if someone has a close encounter with Jesus?"

"I am always on call. But I am usually at home. I don't go where I'm hard to reach, usually. Why don't you have one? Aren't you supposed to be a businessman?"

"I don't even have a *regular* phone, except at the bar."

"You don't have a phone at home?"

"Fuck no. If you want to talk to me you got to call the bar. Better, *come* to the bar, have a drink, and talk like a man."

In the end, they order in a pizza crowded with toppings and wash it down with soda from the vending machine down the hall.

Mule, it is revealed, has grown fussy with age, and slow. The other two have to wait patiently for the bathroom.

Billy is the last one to bed, crawling in next to Meadows, in his skivvies. Mule, by that time, seems already asleep. Billy turns out the light.

After a moment in the darkness, Meadows says, "I wonder about the coffins."

Billy knows what coffins he is talking about.

"What about them?" he says.

"I wonder where they get them. Forty-two in October, eighty-one in November. Twenty-six this month and the month's only half over."

"Jesus, you know the count?" says Billy.

"I got the numbers off the Internet."

"Fuck."

"That's a lot of coffins to have on hand. Where do they get them all from?"

"Probably a base in Germany, my guess. Mule? What do you think?"

"I'm trying to sleep. Thoughts like that will keep you awake."

"They could have a warehouse," says Meadows, "there in Baghdad, full of 'em, so they're always ready."

"Maybe, but they can't be makin' 'em there."

"Why not? Lots of cheap labor."

"No wood. The place looks like Mars."

"They could import the wood. The embargo's over."

"Then they might as well import the finished thing. Germany would be my bet. Good solid craftsmanship."

"Only you're forgetting something. The Germans aren't going along with this war. They're not our friends anymore."

"They'd go along with makin' coffins, though, that's business."

"But what about all the cheap labor?"

"We're not lookin' to save money in Iraq."

"That's true. Seems like we're lookin' to spend money. What is it, billions and billions, more than Bill Gates, even."

"Only it's all our money."

"You gotta spend money to make money."

"But not for us, you can be sure of that. We're not makin' any money."

"It'll trickle down. It always trickles down."

"Yeah, and there'll always be dudes like us, happy with the tricklin' down part."

* * *

The morning breaks cloudy and chilly. Mule feels it in his knees. The pain is not so severe, and yet it is a terrible thing, permanent, a daily reminder of what is lost. Daily, he tries to shake that dread away and remind himself of what is gained through loss:

compassion, resolve, and gratitude for the parts of himself that continue to keep on working. There are no curses, he insists again and again, only blessings in disguise.

Mornings are especially hard and slow-going. That is why he is amazed at, and a bit envious of, Billy's energy and enthusiasm, with his, "Reveille, reveille, reveille, now drop your cocks and grab your socks . . . clean sweep, fore and aft." What a pity some men cannot stay young and in the Navy forever.

In the lobby a continental breakfast is served for guests: weak coffee, dry pastries, underripe fruit.

Billy says, "One of the things I miss most? The chow."

Mule chuckles. Billy has just reinforced his notion. Imagine, missing Navy food.

"I do. I miss the oceans of powerful good coffee, twenty-four/seven. I really miss shit on a shingle—my favorite breakfast to this day, when I can find it—and French toast, fried up potatoes, and at sea in a storm the way those fried eggs run long on the pitching grille. And Naval hospital chow—the best of the best. You ever been in a Navy hospital? You don't know what you missed, man. I was gonna fake a bad back or a heart attack so I could stay in the hospital a little longer."

"You're pathetic," is Mule's observation, though he makes it with a smile.

"No, this civilian chow is pathetic. My memories are full of nourishment, and plenty of it."

"Me, I don't ever want to see another Navy egg," says Mule.

"Well, don't worry, 'cause you won't."

Meadows takes only coffee. Billy is on the brink of asking him about brig food but decides to save that for another time. In some small ways, he has a filter. He knows there were days in the brig of only piss 'n' punk—bread and water. Goes well with the hard labor.

They don't take the time to sit down. They grab a few things at the buffet and balance their breakfasts in one hand, their bags in the other, as they make their way to the Taurus in the parking area.

"When the Twin Towers came down, my first impulse was to get to the base, re-up for the duration."

"For the chow?" says Mule.

"For revenge. I'm an experienced first-class petty officer. I felt I could do something."

"Like what?"

"Like what I used to do, active duty. Only I knew they wouldn't want a dude who can't lift his right arm above his shoulder and needs an afternoon nap."

"You didn't have a nap yesterday afternoon."

"Sure I did. For about fifty miles of the interstate there I was out like a light."

"I can almost believe that."

"Now that I think about it, I needed a nap when I *was* in the Navy. Anyway, what I did instead was I went down there to give a flagon of blood. The lady asked me if I had paid for sex any time during the last six months. Well, like to shit in my flat hat. I told her my philosophy of life."

"That all sex has to be paid for?"

"Verily, padre. I said, 'Lady, listen up, I never had sex I *didn't* pay for, one way or the other.'"

"Did she take your blood anyway?"

"No, she determined I was drunk and sent me away."

"Were you?"

"A little. So all I could do for the war effort was go down to Target and buy a pair of Hush Puppies and three pairs of skivvies. I also gave a hundred to the Red Cross, which I later read in the paper probably went to buy some co-op owner in Tribeca a nice uptown lunch. Disaster ain't what it used to be."

They throw their overnight bags into the trunk.

Meadows asks, "When did you get to pack a bag, Billy? We went right from the bar."

"I always keep a bag in the trunk of my car. Sometimes a lady friend asks me to stay over. I hate to say no."

"Is this one particular lady friend or are there more?" asks Mule.

"One at the moment, but I'm always holding auditions."

"Does she have a name, or do you call her Lady Friend?"

"Gloria. G-L-O-R-I-A." He sings it.

"It's funny," says Meadows. "I had the same reaction."

"Hello?"

Sometimes Meadows is a beat behind the conversation.

"I wished I could enlist too," he says. "But in my case . . . Anyway, Larry went off and joined the Marines, so that was my contribution. I wish he would have joined the Navy instead, but . . . I didn't stop him. 'Course I couldn't have, he would have done it anyway. A kid makes up his own mind. What a bad day, that day."

"It didn't have to happen," says Mule.

"What didn't?" says Meadows. They are talking about two different days.

"The attack on the towers, the Pentagon."

"That's what they say," says Billy, ". . . but you could say that about almost anything. Nothing has to happen, but somehow it always does."

Billy gets behind the wheel. Mule gets into the back seat again.

"I'm not talking about better intelligence," says Mule, "or even paying attention to the intelligence you have, I'm talking about airlines that wouldn't spend the hundred bucks to make sure their cockpit door was secure. You think about it. If those four doors on those four airplanes weren't ever opened, something bad might have happened, but nothing near like what did happen. Hundred dollars would be my bid on the job."

Billy starts the car. "This time the old padre is right, sad to say, more's the pity. There's enough malfeasance to go around . . ."

"Malfeasance?" asks Meadows.

"And nonfeasance both. Mule has got this one correct. You can't get in the cockpit, you can't bring down the towers. You can't bring down nothin', maybe not even the plane."

"Corporations run the country, only a fool doesn't know it," says Mule. "The government's there just to make it easy on the corporations. If they never put people ahead of profits . . ."

"That ain't gonna happen. It ain't in the nature of the beast. Corporations make money and that's all that they do. It's their only purpose. Okay, you know, I can live with that. But the government needs to make sure they don't kill us along the way."

"They are killing us! It's all about the bottom line. They factor in loss of life, misery, as the cost of doing business, and mostly it doesn't cost them. Take the airlines, they counted up three thousand dead and ran the numbers and said, uh-oh, that crossed the line. Because they finally did fix those doors, didn't they?"

"Yeah, those crashes hurt business," Billy says. "People didn't want to fly anymore. That made the cost of securing the doors money well invested."

"Doesn't matter anyway," says Meadows, "because when the airlines get in trouble, the government bails them out. *We* bail them out, the same people they let die to save a few bucks."

"Fuck me," says Billy, "it's another quagmire. We got so many quagmires you don't know where to put your foot down."

Billy pulls the car onto Route One, the road to the base. They drive a while in silence and then he says, "Listen up, what do you make of that cheerleader?"

"Who?"

"The 'Resident.' You like him?"

"No, but that's just personal," says Mule. "I'd like him to be smarter than me. I'd like him to be smarter than *you*."

"Is that an insult?"

"If he can't be smarter, I'd like him to be honest."

"He seems like a decent guy," says Meadows. "Seems sincere to me."

"He reminds me of those ensigns that used to come aboard," says Billy, "just out of OCS or the Academy, all of them told on graduation day, 'Now you are leaders.' And then they tried to tell us that they are leaders, but we knew. Leaders don't go around talking about leadership. They *practice* it. This ain't no war. It's a bloody business transaction."

"And he's no president," says Mule. "He's an appointee appointed by appointees."

They get into the line of cars streaming onto the base. Airmen going on duty, civilians with a base job.

Four

IN THE HANGAR, A MOTHER weeps. She is a young woman herself, dressed simply and neat. She might have younger children still at home, who were not allowed to come here, to endure this with her and her husband. Her hair is red and her face is freckled. Her eyes are red, from crying. She holds a hankie against her face, as though attempting to smother the tears. In a breaking voice, she frets over how they might have "fixed up" her son. She wants him to look nice. Her husband, though, is angry. He has a full head of hair and a thick neck and strong arms. A working man. He tells her not to think about it. What's coming is nothing but remains, just the broken shell of what used to be their boy, their firstborn. She doesn't listen. She says, "Maybe they can crack the lid a little, just so I can hold his hand."

"Dammit, honey," her husband whispers harshly, "it ain't gonna be him, I tell you, that's not gonna be the boy who walked out of our house. That's not gonna be our Tommy."

Another group of four—mother, father, second husband, second wife—huddle together, waiting, all their past animosities and accusations forgotten. One more circle—a triangle really—waits, a mother and father and grown daughter, whose rage burns on her face. He was her twin, the other half of her, and he was her best friend. Three families, of much different sorts, grieving over the very same thing. Then there is the other group, not a family at all, just three aging veterans with no more history together than the four and a half days they journeyed toward a prison, over thirty years ago.

The hangar is cold and hollow and cheerless. A folding table has been set up with a coffee mess and doughnuts. Only Billy partakes, at first. Then the father who was angry with his wife for thinking their son was coming home and he thinking it was not their son, not anymore, not even bearing a resemblance to what he thought of as their son, joins him, accepting that not only are grief and coffee not mutually exclusive, they are naturally linked.

The other man says to Billy, who is returning for his second cup, "At least they caught the son of a bitch. It wasn't in vain."

It takes Billy a moment to peg the son of a bitch he's talking about. He wants to tell the man it is in vain, that "did not die in vain" is just a phrase they use to keep the war rolling. Did those fifty thousand young men *not* die in vain in Vietnam? Was it them and their sacrifice that kept the dominoes from falling, that stemmed the spread of communism throughout the world, which every freedom-loving American was assured would happen should North Vietnam swallow up the south? What can you say that is real to a father who needs to justify losing his son in a war that is undeclared, a war with no clear purpose, or rather purposes that change as each preceding one is revealed to be hollow? Good to fight a tyrant. A tyrant becomes purpose enough then, after the lie is revealed: we must slay the monster and free the people. The world, however, has never lacked for tyrants. What now, now that the monster is bagged? Is it over? Was it worth it? This father never had that question put to him as a choice: the foreign tyrant for your son's life. The commander in chief has not sacrificed a child, nor has any assenting senator or congressman. Nor have any of their friends. Only poor broken men like Meadows and this other father.

Billy nods and says, "Yeah, they got him all right, the son of a bitch."

The hangar door slides open to the chilly and cloudy morning and two officers stride in, each holding a clipboard. One is an Army major, the other a Marine light colonel. Behind them come the flag-covered coffins, on what look like large children's wagons.

Billy leaves his coffee cup on the table and goes back to Meadows and Mule.

"They're not even wood, are they?" says Meadows.

They are not. They are fabricated of aluminum and look like oversized foot lockers. An enlisted man stands at attention next to each coffin.

The somber officers direct parents to their loved ones.

The major has three. Only the fourth is a Marine, Meadows' son.

"Mr. Meadows . . . ?" The colonel addresses Billy.

"No, it's him." He nods to Meadows, who stands dumbly, his eyes on the flag-covered aluminum box that he knows contains his son.

The colonel shakes Meadows's hand and says, "Mr. Meadows, the President of the United States has asked me to express his deep regret that your son was killed in action."

"Sure he has," grumbles Billy, loud enough to be heard. Certainly, the colonel hears him. Mule shoots Billy a look: don't start up. Not here, not now.

"Lance Corporal Meadows died a hero in the service of his country. He was an inspiration to his fellow Marines."

The escort stands at stony attention. He is a young black man no more than twenty. Also a lance corporal. Something is wrong with his left ear lobe. It is covered with tiny bumps and looks like it is rotting away.

"Your loved one has been designated to be buried with full military honors at the National Cemetery in Arlington," the colonel goes on. "I am authorized to make those arrangements, at your convenience, sir."

"Can I see him?"

"That would not be advisable, sir,"

"Oh . . . is it against the rules?"

"Trust me on this. You don't want to see him."

"I do, though. I have to."

"Mr. Meadows . . . the Lance Corporal was hit in the back of the head. I can assure you he felt no pain . . . but the exit wound in such a case is devastating . . . to the face."

"They were *behind* him?" Meadows asks. "They shot him from behind?"

"Remember him as he was," says Mule.

Meadows seems to be considering it. He looks to Billy, asking without words, waiting for him to say something.

"You can always remember him the way he was," says Billy, "no matter what. I'd have to see him, but that's me. The important thing is, you don't have to listen to no Marine colonel anymore. Those days are gone."

The young Marine enlisted man doesn't move but his dark eyes twitch. The colonel looks like he would love to put a lethal move on the mouthy old man.

"I'm gonna see my boy," said Meadows, "one last time."

"As you wish," says the colonel, then turns to Billy and Mule. "Are you family?"

"We're not related," says Mule.

The colonel orders the Marine, "Washington, escort these two gentlemen to the coffee mess. Mr. Meadows, I will lift and hold the lid. You tell me when to lower it."

Washington leads Billy and Mule away. He can hardly contain himself. "Man, you stuck it to the colonel," he says.

"Colonels don't scare me, kid," says Billy. "Never have, never will. Light colonels even less."

"You a Marine?"

"Bite your tongue. US Navy, retired."

"Swabby? All up in the colonel's face? The colonel's used to being right."

"That don't mean he is. Listen up, why don't you as you were or somethin', you're givin' me a stiff neck."

The Marine smiles and relaxes.

"What's the skinny on your ear?" Billy asks him. "It's pretty gnarly."

"Baghdad boil."

"Huh?"

"Everybody's got one. Don't worry, it's not catchy. You have to be bit by a teeny sand fly they got over there. It's got a parasite. They say it'll go away in a year or two."

"Fuck me. One of the little bonuses of invading a country you don't know shit about."

"This is a mistake," says Mule.

"What?"

He is looking at Meadows, who first braces himself, then buckles at the knees when the coffin lid is lifted. He grips the side of the coffin for support.

"Jesus . . . I hope not."

"Did you want him to see his son's mutilated body or did you just want to out-tough a Marine colonel?"

"I didn't want anything. I'm just along for the ride."

The other families seeing one coffin open now demand that their coffin lids be lifted as well.

"You're, like, all friends?" asks the young Marine.

"I wouldn't go that far," says Mule.

"It's what you call a complicated relationship," says Billy.

"Don't tell me," says the Marine, "you're not the dudes who took Meadows's father to the brig, are you?"

Both Billy and Mule are stunned.

"You *are!* Fuck me."

"You *know* about that?" asks Mule.

"Fuckin' A. I was Larry's best friend in the unit. I knew the whole story. You took him to the brig and it took you, like, *five days?* You whored and drank your way up there? A wild white dude and a worried black one?"

"Worried?"

"We did some stuff," says Billy. "You're tellin' me his kid knew all about that, told you about it?"

"Yeah, sure I knew. No one else knew anything about his old man. Until the end . . . just before he went down."

"You were with him, in the ambush?"

"Ambush?"

"Wasn't it an ambush?"

"If you want to call it that."

"Well, that's what they're callin' it, an ambush and a fire fight." Washington quickly scans the hangar. Everyone is lost in his own grief. The colonel's face betrays a little self-satisfaction.

"If that's what they're saying it was, then that's what it was."

"But what was it, really?"

"Larry . . . Larry fucked up. He just fucked up."

* * *

Me and Meadows and three other guys were manning a Humvee and humping school supplies.

School supplies?

Tablets, pencils, rulers, a couple Hewlett-Packard computers, some new books because they had to get rid of the old shit and tell a different story now. Shit like that. We were delivering the shit to all the schools that were reopening. We were at it all day long. It was 1500 hours and we were on our last run of the day. There was the usual bitching going on. We'd rather be killing Iraqis than working UPS, that kind of bitch, even though there wasn't one man on that Hummer had ever killed anybody. Yet. Then we did a bitch about the heat and the sand up our ass and the cold and the sand up our ass again. Hated that fuckin' sand. You could run an all-day bitch just about the sand. One of the guys made the crack he wished he was in the fuckin' Navy. He was only trying to get a rise out of us, which he did, but there was some truth to it. We knew the Navy had it best. They got three hots and a cot, no sand up the ass, piped in music, hot showers. Then we started dissin' the swabbies, calling them pussies, chickens of the sea, like that. Meadows said, hey, my old man was a swabby, he loved the Navy. Then they all ragged him and felt sorry for him to have to go through life with that kind of abuse in his background. Somebody asked him how long his old man put in, and Meadows said, nine years, eight of them in the brig. Everybody laughed but I knew it was true. Like I said, we were best friends. He was embarrassed that his dad had been a major fuck-up, a brig bird, and left the service with a DD. But he was also kinda proud that his father done his time like a man and he held his mud, thanks to the two Shore Patrol chasers who escorted him to prison. One, a white signalman, the other a black gunner's mate. Meadows had some mixed emotions about his dad. Everybody who joins the Corps has a reason. That was his, I think.

The driver stopped outside this little store, Abdul's gedunk, we called it. We'd stopped there earlier, in the morning. It was my turn to make the Coke run, but Meadows said he'd do it. I said, no, I could do it. He goes, no, I gotta get outa this vehicle 'cause everybody's fartin' all the time. I go, okay, but lemme give you some cash for the Cokes. He didn't even wait for that. He was gone. So we kicked back and waited for him.

He was a big dude, six four. Strong dude. You couldn't miss him. He double-timed it across the street to Abdul's. He left his piece in the vehicle with us. We were talking some shit, I don't know what, when I hear this Arab shout out something. I can't give it to you in the Arabic, but I know the translation. Who doesn't? God is great. It's their fuckin' motto. I look out and see Meadows. His fingers were laced around the necks of five Coke bottles, and behind him this raghead shouting God is great and putting a cap in the back of Meadow's head. That quick. Nothin' you could do. I yelled and we just lit up that fuckin' place. We killed the raghead, we killed Abdul, we killed all his family and all his customers. Whoever was in or around that gedunk got lit up with the raghead. I was for lightin' up the whole fuckin' 'hood. We pulled Meadows back into the Hummer and went home. Fuck a whole bunch of school supplies.

* * *

"He fucked up. Larry just fucked up."

"How did he fuck up?"

"Didn't have his piece. Left his piece behind. Shoulda had his piece with him."

"What good would that have done?"

"Shouldn't of gone on the Coke run. It wasn't his fuckin' turn. It was my turn."

"But then you would have got killed."

"I wouldn't fuck up, though."

"How would you not fuck up?"

"I woulda brought my fuckin' piece."

"What good would that have done?"

"I woulda wasted the fucker."

"You wouldn't have seen him, just like Larry didn't see him. You would have been carrying the Cokes, just like Larry was."

"No, man, I woulda wasted him."

It is only a sham tragedy when the son of a sailor becomes a Marine, something the father can share with his buddies down at the tavern. The joke is on him, where did he go wrong? The fear is real, though, when the son is sent off to combat for manufactured reasons in a fierce and naked terrain. What do you call it when the son is killed there, not fighting in defense of his homeland but delivering school supplies to children who will be taught to hate him, not killed in combat but murdered in religious hatred, not by an enemy soldier protecting his own homeland but by a zealot in the name of his God? And what is it when the father is not told the truth but a charitable lie? Why not tell the truth, always, unless it is to feed the Big Lie with smaller falsehoods, no matter how well-meaning?

"I'm from Oakland, California," says Washington, the young black Marine. "Any weekend of the year, I can expect somebody to put a cap in my ass, but this sucks. And they took him away so fast. Most of the guys in the unit didn't even know he was dead till evening chow and the scuttlebutt got around. They just swept him away. No one had a chance to even, like, say good-bye. Except for me."

Across the hangar, Meadows nods and the colonel lowers the lid. Meadows does not move away.

"He's supposed to get the Silver Star out of this," says Billy.

"Oh, he'll get the Star. We'll all get the Star. The more Silver Stars the better."

"We cannot tell Meadows about this," says Mule. "Not now."

"When?"

"Not ever. Let him have his Silver Star, his burial at Arlington with military honors. Let him have his hero. Lord knows he's had little enough in his life."

"You mean, let him swallow their lie."

"What's more important?"

"I don't know. The truth?"

"Nothing can be gained by telling him," Mule says.

"Some things shouldn't have to be gained. They should just *be* there."

Billy walks toward the coffin, toward Meadows and the colonel.

"It's not your son," says Mule, trailing behind him, slowed by his canes.

"But if it was . . ." says Billy.

The Marine takes Mule's arm and they move a little faster that way. "It's not your place to say anything. Let it go, Billy."

As they come within earshot, they can hear the colonel saying, "There is always a sound reason for my recommendations. I'm sorry, sir, but I did warn you."

Meadows is trembling, unable to speak. Billy puts a hand on his shoulder. Meadows turns and goes into Billy's arms. Billy holds him. He can't remember when last, if ever, he held a man like this. He pats his back.

"Billy . . . he don't have a face anymore," Meadows whimpers.

Billy doesn't know what to say. All he has to offer is the universal spine stiffener, God's blessing and curse combined: "You gotta be a man."

Meadows nods into his shoulder and stands back, runs a handkerchief over his face.

Billy stares down the Marine officer. "Colonel, maybe it would help, a little, to know exactly how this boy died."

The fake civility does not fool the colonel.

"The Lance Corporal acquitted himself with dignity and honor and he died a hero."

"Yeah, well, they're all heroes, ain't they?"

"That they are."

"All heroes, for sure. But what was the scene? How did it happen that he was shot in the back of the head? Like a dog."

"I don't have all the details."

"Some of them, then. Anything. Just so he knows."

"I would like to know," says Meadows, through tears.

"He was a brave Marine, a credit to the Corps, and he served his country well."

"I'm sure he did. So did we all. And we still have to, when we get the chance."

"Without question."

Billy nods, letting it go. "Okay."

"What's goin' on, Billy?" asks Meadows.

"Nothing," he says.

"We should talk about the funeral," says Mule.

"We can make those arrangements now," says the colonel.

"Billy?" Meadows asks again.

"I'd just want to know," he says. "I'd want everybody to know. If it was my son was a hero, I'd want to know who shot him in the back of the head and why. I'd want to talk to somebody who was there with him, at the end."

"Yeah," says Meadows. "They weren't all killed, were they? Or else they'd be here with him. Where are the others? Why's my boy the only Marine here? There oughta be somebody was there who's still alive."

"I was there," says the young Marine, Washington.

The colonel shoots him a look, but it's too late now. The bereaved father is staring into Washington's eyes.

"Washington," says the colonel, "tell the Lance Corporal's father what happened."

Washington takes a deep breath.

* * *

Outside the hangar is a public phone. Mule is on it, talking to his wife, trying to stay warm in the chilly air. Monday is wash day. She is doing the household laundry, and for Mule it should be a day off, or as close as he gets to one. He should be with his feet up, listening to Nina Simone and reading scripture, preparing a sermon.

"Yes, it is a lie," Mule tells his wife. "A lie is always a lie, but this is not the first nor the last coming out of that war, out of that godforsaken country. What truth do you expect to find in war? That you've got to win? Even that's not true. We lost in Vietnam. Yes, they lie to make heroes. Heroes inspire. Nobody wants a Marine gunned down makin' a Coke run while delivering school supplies. But dead is dead. Meadows didn't need to know that. It's tearing him up inside. . . . I tried to help, believe me, but he keeps saying they took his son's face. Not his life, but his face. Does the truth set you free? I don't know anymore, I don't see it happening here. . . . We're all just standing around waiting, I don't know what for. Oh, one way or another this will turn out to be the Billy Bad-Ass show. That man's a menace. He can't keep his mouth shut if he's up to his nose in shit. . . . I'm sorry, sweetheart. . . . I know, I know. . . . Short of coming up behind him and braining him with my cane, I don't know what I can do. He was brained once already over thirty years ago, I was there, and looks like it didn't even turn him sideways."

Mule hobbles back into the hangar to see Meadows leaning back against the coffin, both hands on it, almost protectively, his head down, looking at no one.

"Where are we with this?" Mule asks Billy.

"Where we was, pretty much. He wants his son's face back."

"I don't know why I came, except that you bullied me into it. There's very little I can do here. I want to go home."

"You quittin'?"

"Quitting what? Just what are we supposed to be doing here?"

"We'll know in another minute or two."

"You never could leave well enough alone, could you?"

"Never found well enough, though I keep on lookin'. Yo, Meadows."

Meadows looks up at him.

"I think a gesture is called for, kid."

Meadows nods and stands up straight. He turns to the colonel. "You can take your Arlington cemetery and all your honors and your flags and you can—"

"Lad," says Mule, "easy now. Out of respect for your son . . ."

Meadows nods again, taking all counsel, but finally holding his own on what he says next.

"Colonel, I'm takin' Larry home. You can't have him no more."

Billy nods his head, assenting in somber tribute.

"I assure you that is a bad decision and you will regret it," says the colonel.

Meadows doesn't answer, if he even hears him. He tries to push the coffin on its wheels toward the hangar's open doors. It does not roll easily.

"Hold on," says the colonel. "We will transport the body, at no expense to you. Anywhere you choose."

"I'm takin' him home."

"And I'm gonna help you," says Billy, and together they push the coffin. It rolls better now.

"I'm sorry, but I cannot release the body, except to a licensed mortician or a clergyman."

"I guess that would be me," says Mule. He walks with his two canes and follows the other two to the door and beyond.

Washington is left alone with the colonel. He has been expecting a sound reaming, at the least, and now might be the time for that, but the colonel does not yet turn his attention to him. He looks at the three old veterans pushing the government-issue coffin.

"Just where in the huckleberry hell do those old fools think they're going?"

"Home . . . he said, sir."

* * *

It has not warmed up at all, still in the mid-forties out on the parking lot, with dark clouds hanging over. The walk and the pushing, however, have made them warm, and anger can create heat as well. What stopped the walk and the push and even the anger was the passenger side of the Taurus, which now has a hamburger-sized dent in the fender. Though it is of no consequence, they examine the dent, drawn to the small distraction as old men are wont to do. This can't be rubbed out. The paint is cracked. Rust is sure to set in. No matter, Billy says, rust is no big thing. Meadows feels responsible for it. Billy explains that he has a customer who works in a body shop and one of these days he is going to go over to his place of employment and have him take care of everything marring the cosmetics of his little car. Meadows insists on paying for it. Billy tells him forget about it, he doesn't care, honestly. He has no pride of ownership. Maybe once with the bar, in the beginning, for about a week. Then he was over it.

"That was a mighty fine gesture, lad," says Mule. "Now what?"

"Oh, there's no turning back," says Billy.

"I was talking to the lad."

"This is a courageous gesture," says Billy, "your son would be proud."

"Do you think so?" says Meadows. "I'd like him to be proud of me, I don't think he ever was."

"Sure he was. That young Marine said he was."

The young Marine named Washington watches them from the open door of the hangar, where he has been ordered to stand by. He does not know why, but that is the way it is with most orders. He does not mind waiting this out. He has no heart for anything else at the moment.

"Really?" says Meadows. "How'd he know?"

"He was best friends with your boy, who told him so."

"Really? And Larry said he was proud of me?"

"Your boy was also proud of the Corps," says Mule. "There's no denying that. Wouldn't he want to be buried at Arlington?"

"Yeah, what about that?" adds Billy, but Mule knows this is not support for a reasonable turnaround. Billy is so confident that he can waltz them all through chaos that he's willing to pretend to look at all sides first.

"I know my Larry. He wouldn't want no Silver Stars or to be called a hero when all he was was a poor kid doin' what he wasn't trained for in a place where he had no right to be. He wouldn't want to be lied about. So I'm takin' him home with me. I was always proud of *him*."

"You're overpowered by your own emotions, lad," says Mule. "Think about this. How're you going to get him home? You gonna strap that coffin to the roof of Billy's car?"

"We could do that," says Billy. "We'd need some help liftin' it up."

"Don't be ridiculous," says Mule.

"Why not? Tell me a better way to be. You *wish* you could be ridiculous. You wish somebody could teach you, but it's too late now."

"Let the government take care of the transport, Meadows," says Mule. "They owe you that, and that's what they're good at."

"I don't like the government right now," says Meadows.

"You don't have to."

"I'm mad at them."

"Of course you are."

"I don't trust 'em either."

"That mistrust is not misplaced," says Mule. "I understand all that, but face the reality of the situation here."

"We could rent a U-Haul," Billy says.

"Sure," says Meadows. "We could do that. It's a long way, though."

"Not all that far," says Billy.

"And I don't like the idea of Larry ridin' in the back of a truck."

"Kids love ridin' in the backs of trucks. I always did."

"That's true," says Meadows.

"This is insane," says Mule.

"I had a pickup," Meadows remembers, "an old Dodge Ram . . . Larry used to love to ride in the back of that thing."

"Even takin' it easy," says Billy, "we'd be there before dark tomorrow, 'cause today's half shot by the time we get goin'."

"We could drive all night."

"Whoa. As long as you're doin' the drivin'," says Billy. "I don't see so good at night."

"Let's do it. Mule 'n' me'll stay here, you can take the car and go find a truck." Meadows gives him his envelope full of cash. "Pay for it out of this."

"Consider it done," says Billy. "One truck, comin' up."

"I'll be going with Billy," says Mule.

"Good idea. I get lost."

"You can drop me off at the bus station. I'll be going back home now."

For a moment no one says anything.

"I've had enough, I believe," says Mule.

"I understand, Mule, I'm sorry I dragged you up here."

"I thought we were going to a funeral. I thought I could be of some help."

"We *are* going to a funeral," says Billy. "It's just gonna take a little longer to get there."

"I'm sorry, lad."

"That's okay, Mule. I'm just glad I got to see you again."

Mule loops one cane over his forearm and extends his hand. Meadows shakes it, then gives him a hug, awkwardly trapping his canes against him.

"Shipmates forever," Meadows whispers.

"God bless you," Mule says.

* * *

For the first few moments in the car, neither man speaks, but Billy is an old signalman and he cannot go long without communication, not that the silence wasn't sending messages.

"You know," he says, "I'm surprised you made it this far."

"You make it sound like a marathon. It may yet turn out to be one, I suppose."

"You commit to the first step, you gotta commit to all of them."

"We should stop and ask somebody where the bus station is."

"It's a small town, we'll run into it. Give you a few more minutes to enjoy my company."

"Always a pleasure."

"So what's on your agenda? Read the Bible on the way home, leftover ham for dinner, check nobody's broke into the church and swiped the communion wine, say a little prayer?"

"Oh, I'll say a little prayer long before that. The bigger question, what's on your agenda?"

"Help a dude I feel I owe one. Nothin' more, nothin' less."

"Even he says you don't owe him a thing."

"All the more reason."

"What would have happened, way back then, if we had taken that kid directly to prison? No talk, no side trips, no trying to show him a good time."

"He woulda got there three days earlier—and been released three days earlier—with nothin' to remember in between. And we woulda wound up feeling like good little cops."

Before they can find the bus station, they come upon a Ryder agency. Billy parks on the street, half a block away. He takes the bags from the trunk and carries them all.

"I can carry my own bag," says Mule.

Billy ignores him and continues with all the bags to the agency, Mule hobbling behind.

The clerk is somebody's wife, and has been since she was eighteen, probably the owner's, because her proprietary air reveals her to be more than an employee. She smokes a cigarette as she waits on them. She has a van, she says, that would work for them, but they might prefer a truck with a hydraulic tail lift. Billy likes that idea, even though it is far more than they need. That lift sounds very appealing, could come in handy, he believes, and on the road, bigger is better.

"What'll you be hauling?" she asks.

"Well . . ." Billy hesitates, then decides not to tell her. ". . . your truck with the lift'll handle it."

"Will you be dropping off the vehicle at another location or returning it here?"

Billy hadn't thought about that. Damn, once in Portsmouth, what then? He probably could fly back . . . to where? Philly, Baltimore, then make his way somehow back here, unless there's a flight to Wilmington, which would be a little easier, or the train. Either way, a one-way ticket is going to cost, and he can't let Meadows pay for it, even if he'd have that much left of his stash after they're through with all this.

"Don'cha know?" she asks.

"I'm gonna return it here," says Billy.

"When will that be?"

Again, he is stumped. This sort of thing, as he knows from experience, can turn out to take longer than expected.

"Better give me a week."

"A week?" says Mule. "Oh, boy."

Somebody's wife looks uneasily at Mule and taps away at her keyboard.

"Is this going to take very long?" asks Mule.

"Now, Mule, why don't you just sit down and take a load off. When we're done, we're done."

Mule makes his way to one of the two vinyl and chrome chairs.

Somebody's wife is growing more and more suspicious. Two old guys walk in off the street, carrying bags. One white, indecisive and vague. One black, impatient and infirm. And referred to as "Mullah." That's an Arabic thing, isn't it? That's an Arabic cleric. A black Muslim. The Mullah. The Holy Mullah. She's heard it before, somewhere.

She frets inwardly. They always pick Ryder.

"I'll need to see your driver's license," she says.

"Yes, ma'am."

The white guy fumbles through his pockets. Doesn't he have a wallet, like normal people? She hopes he doesn't even have a license. No license, no truck.

He pulls a fist out of one pocket and drops change and keys and something small and strange, a black square with a blade in the center. Like a tiny guillotine that the French used to use to cut off people's heads, like that Marie Antoinette bitch who wanted everybody to eat her cake. It's only a little thing but it scares her because she doesn't know how it works. The old guy brings his other fist out of the other pocket and drops some cash and cards and hard candy. He fishes through the cards and comes up with a driver's license.

She examines it carefully.

"Virginia, huh?"

"Yes, ma'am."

"What brings you up here?"

"Well . . . excuse me, young lady, but is that any business of yours?"

"Just making conversation. Trying to be friendly."

"I am here because of a death in the family."

"Oh . . . I'm sorry."

"That's all right." He smiles. "It wasn't my family."

There is something not right with this old guy.

"Will you be the only driver?"

This is turning out to be more complicated than he anticipated. He has found the vehicle he wants, now he wants to be off with it. No way is he going to be the only driver, especially if they're moving at night. Meadows is going to have to drive too. He will take a turn at the wheel, but no way is he doing all the driving. "I'll have some help," he says.

"Then I'll need to see the other driver's license."

"What other driver's license?"

"Of the other driver. Is it that gentleman there?"

"The Mule? The Mule can hardly walk, let alone handle a big rig."

There it is again. *The Mullah*. The frail spiritual leader, there's always one of them, either blind or lame. He looks like a country preacher, but he could easily be of the Nation of Islam, wherever the hell that is.

"Well, whoever," she says, "I'll still need their licenses."

"No, I'm gonna drive it myself."

"So now you *are* the only driver?"

"Yes ma'am, I be the wheelman."

*Wheel*man? Somebody's wife can take care of herself, but she is beginning to have some fears for her safety.

"Insurance on the vehicle?"

"What about it?"

"Would you like to get some?"

"No, ma'am, not necessary."

I'll just *bet* it's not necessary. "How would you like to pay for this?" she asks.

"Cash," says Billy, putting the brown envelope on the counter.

Cash! That tears it. She gives him a truck, it's the last she sees of it, for sure.

The old man counts it out, in twenties, tens, fives, and singles. To be fair, it's not like she has never made a cash transaction before, with or without insurance coverage. Poor white trash forced to move have occasionally come in with their garage sale proceeds, in an envelope, just like his. But this is different. Somebody's wife has a very bad feeling about this, these two, the silent Mullah and the evasive wheelman. She would love to make them go away. Call it a gut feeling. Her husband, however, has no gut feelings and does not like them in her. Besides, if she's wrong these old coots could be back with a shyster lawyer hot to file an anti-discrimination suit against her. So go ahead, take the fucking truck, blow it up, blow up the world for all I care.

Once good to go, Billy asks, "There is one more thing you can do for us. Can you direct us to the bus station?

Bus station? You just picked up a truck, what do you need a bus for? She directs them, in spite of her misgivings. They would have found it anyway. They're probably going to blow it up.

* * *

Billy has to help Mule get into the truck. It is a bit of a climb for him. Then he goes to the other side and settles in himself. He puts his hands on either side of the steering wheel, grasps it firmly, sits up straight.

"Sixteen or sixty-six," he says, "put a man behind the wheel of a big rig and he feels like hot shit. This is gonna be fun!"

"It's a rented truck with an automatic transmission."

"Bigger 'n' anything you ever handled."

"And it's not supposed to be fun. This is a solemn occasion. A boy is dead."

"But we're still alive, with time tickin' fast away. If there's a minute comes up that's not too terrible, I'm gonna try to enjoy it." He starts up the truck and pulls away. "I remember you as a guy being up for some fun."

"I still am, as long as the fun is right in God's eyes."

"God's eyes! God don't have any eyes."

"Oh, he's got eyes, and ears too. He hears every insult you send his way, and there will be a reckoning. You might have got away with your insubordination in the Navy, but there will be no talking your way out of the Captain's Mast in the sky."

Billy laughs. "If it comes to that, I'm gonna stand at attention and say to God, You could have fooled me. You *did* fool me.

Where were You when they were selling slaves, raping children, pourin' innocent God-fearing folks into mass graves? Where were You when Your priests went around the world, torturing and slaughtering whole races of people who never heard of You and didn't want to? Where were You later when Your priests were forcing little boys to have sex with them, and then protecting themselves when the truth came out? And where were You when they flew airplanes down into the city, killing thousands of folks just goin' to work, and the murderers shouting Your name or You by another name? When it comes to that, where were You when my friend's kid was buying soda and a raghead killed him in Your name, or that other name, same difference. Where were You? You see, I'm not gonna explain myself to *God*, He's gonna have to explain Himself to *me*. And I guarantee you at the end of it, if He exists at all, He's gonna say, 'Get your ass in here, you're my kind of dude.'"

Mule is rendered silent by his sacrilege, his divine effrontery.

"At least," Billy adds, "that's what I'm hopin'. If he's a tight-ass kind of God, I'm fucked."

"I'll pray for your soul, Billy. I'll get my congregation to pray too, you're gonna need all the help I can get."

"Where were You, I could say, when the politicians used Your name to bless themselves and their secret deals."

"Okay, okay, I get it. Can we just find that bus station now?"

Billy drives slow, looking at street signs. At a stop sign he makes a discovery.

"Hey! It's got a radio."

He turns it on and gets the last renter's station: rap, cranked up high. He fumbles for the volume control.

"Turn that shit off," says the Reverend Mulhall.

A car waiting for them to move honks its horn.

Billy opens the window and yells, "Fuck you, asshole!" before pulling away. He doesn't turn it off, but he does lower the volume. He wants to hear some of this.

"Hip hop," he says, as though that says it all. "If you don't like being called jungle bunny you ought not invent something and call it hip hop."

"I didn't invent it. And I invite you not to use terms like that. Next one you get my cane in your face."

"Your people, is my meaning. Now, I've been known to get in a face or two, but even I find some of this stuff offensive. And hard to dance to. Or whistle with. Don't it make you feel a little ashamed to be a black man?"

"No, not really."

"Well, it ought to, dignified old gentleman like you."

"Why should I feel ashamed? This dude is white."

"The fuck!"

"That's affirmative, white as rice."

"No way!"

"Way. Honky born and bred."

"That's comin' out of a white mouth?"

"White sewer mouth."

"Then, by God, I ought to feel ashamed myself. Only I never did identify with the white race."

"This ought to be good. What race do you identify with?"

"Navy blue. That's the only culture ever made any sense to me, till everything kinda went south. Till that fuckin' detail. That didn't happen, I would have made chief, run my own division. I coulda had another ten, fifteen years. Life could have been a lot different. But . . . that's that. You ever miss it?"

"Not for a minute."

"I don't believe that."

"Then don't."

"Why'd you join in the first place?"

"Why did I join the Navy? I grew up in Louisiana in the fifties, *that's* why I joined the Navy. It wasn't all that easy, either. They wanted me as a steward. I was okay with serving this country, I wasn't okay with serving coffee. But a shipboard chief saw something in me he liked and I was designated a gunner's mate striker."

"Well, see, you got a break from a white man."

"I didn't want any break from a white man. What I want is a white boy getting a break from a black man."

"Then let's start with you. Gimme a fuckin' break."

"There's the bus station," says Mule.

Billy pulls into the parking lot.

"You can drop me off here," says Mule.

"No, I'm gonna take you in, make sure you don't get lost."

"I think I can find my own way, thank you. Meadows will be wondering what happened to you."

"I'd better see you off. Who knows when we'll bump into each other again?"

"Maybe never."

"Time being what it is."

Billy carries Mule's bag and waits with it while Mule buys a ticket. He has not been in a bus station for a long time. It all comes back to him, the musty air, the sad-ass people, the garbled announcements. They started by bus, back then, with Meadows in handcuffs. Other sailors waiting for buses turned their heads away, embarrassed by two chasers and a prisoner. Billy told

Meadows he could use the bathroom, but one of them would have to go with him. The kid said he wasn't going to kill himself. Billy sure knew that much. Escape had never entered the kid's mind. Not even that kind. They drank coffee out of Styrofoam cups, leaning against some lockers, away from the others, as well as they could get away from others in a bus station.

Now they are away from themselves. At least it feels that way.

Mule hobbles back with his ticket in hand.

"No problem?"

"Not unless being stuck on a bus for the next eight hours is a problem. Leaves in twenty minutes."

"They're real nice now. Recliners, a shitter. Maybe you'll meet some poor bastard and save his soul."

"I'm hoping I can sleep. I didn't sleep well last night."

"The mattress?"

"I'm too used to my own bed."

"I don't sleep so good either. Remember when we could sleep anywhere, anytime? Remember when you could sleep on a pitching ship with the next rack eight inches from your nose?"

"You can't go back, Billy."

"I know that."

"You can't redo the choices you made, you can only learn from them and make better choices in the future."

"That kind of talk crosses my eyes."

"I'm serious. You got to get over that last detail."

"I was over it the minute I walked away from that brig."

"Sure you were. You've been replaying it ever since then, doing something different this time."

"Haven't thought about it in over thirty years, not until the kid showed up. Jesus . . . and then his dead son."

"Now you want to run the detail again, Norfolk to Portsmouth. You're hoping that this time you get it right. Well, I got news for you, we got it right the last time."

"Okay," says Billy.

"But you're still gonna do it. You're gonna take this boy and his dead son up to Portsmouth and try to make it *fun*."

"You ought to come with."

"Can't do that."

Billy rises to his feet. "Then I'd better get started." He extends his hand and they shake. "I still can't believe it, you a preacher. How's that feel?"

"Pretty good, Billy. It feels pretty good."

"Yeah. Don't ever forget what it feels like to have a friend."

* * *

In his bag Mule carries a small suede-bound Bible, and during moments such as these, waiting for a bus, he likes to open it at random and seek some relevance to the moment. Stumble and ye shall find. It always works.

The book falls open to Deuteronomy and Mule has an impulse to try again, but that would be cheating, so he lets his arthritic finger drop to, "When you are living in the towns that the Lord your God gives you, you may hear that some worthless people of your nation have misled the people of their town to worship gods that you never have worshipped before. If you hear of such a rumor, investigate thoroughly; and if it is true that this evil thing did happen, then kill all the people in that town and all their livestock too. Destroy that town completely. Bring together all the possessions of the people who live there and pile them up in the town square. Then burn the town and everything in it as an offering to the Lord your God. It must be left in ruins forever and never again be rebuilt."

A man in a cheap wrinkled raincoat is talking to the ticket agent. Another man in a black anorak takes a seat near Mule. Mule looks up from his Bible and says hello. He notices the raincoat man now whose back is to him: the ticket agent's eyes dart to Mule.

"Taking a bus today?" asks anorak, distracting him, all for the better since the biblical passage has disturbed him. Some small talk might be refreshing.

"Yes, the bus to Richmond. And you?"

"Richmond, huh. That home for you?"

"No, but it's getting close."

Now cheap raincoat is standing before Mule.

"So you're the one they call the Mullah," he says.

"The what?"

"The Mullah."

"Excuse me," says Mule. "I'm waiting for a bus, reading the Scriptures."

Anorak changes seats, taking the one next to Mule. He looks at the book on Mule's lap. "The Bible? Checking out the competition?"

"Who are you two? What do you want from me?"

"That depends."

"You don't look like thieves, and I don't look like someone who has anything worth stealing, which I don't, so either leave me be or make yourselves clear."

"We're from Homeland Security."

"Say what?"

"Where is William Buddusky of Norfolk, Virginia, right now?"

"Who?" For the instant he honestly doesn't know who the man is talking about.

"You know who. Your wheelman."

"Buddusky? Bad-Ass? Billy Bad-Ass?"

"That his *nom de guerre?*"

"What in the world are you talking about?"

"You're not gonna make that bus," says black anorak. "Possible you won't be home for a long time."

"Am I under arrest for something?"

"Not necessarily."

To Mule, who is already far more tired than he cares to be, this is taking on the aspects of a nightmare.

"You think I'm a threat to Homeland Security?" he asks, mystified. "Look at me."

"Yeah. You see a little girl in dark flowing clothes, eyes that just suck you in, or *off*, metaphorically speaking, and you wonder what's behind the veil. You never see the vest loaded with explosives."

"You think I'm a terrorist?"

"That's what we're trying to find out. Why do they call you the Mullah?"

"They do no such thing. They call me Mule. At least Billy Bad-Ass still does, or did when he rented that truck. I am Reverend Richard Mulhall. Mulhall. In the Navy, it was easier to say Mule."

"You want to tell us about the truck?"

"Oh, yes, I'll tell you all about the truck and its cargo. You're such idiots."

"Yes, sir, we're the idiots that stand between three hundred million Americans and the religious fanatics pledged to kill them."

"God save us."

"God is great," says anorak, sarcastically.

"Where's the truck, old man?"

"Right now? Dover Air Force Base."

Which information has the effect of a hand grenade. Raincoat falls back reaching for his cell phone; anorak twists Mule around, sending his canes and Bible flying, slapping on cuffs in one deft and well-practiced move.

* * *

The young Marine, Washington, remains at his post, standing by, as ordered. So much of his time-in has been spent standing by, an important function he has come to master. He watches the Ryder truck arrive and pull up to where the old guy's Ford had been, that parking place now occupied by Larry in his casket. He can see Larry's father talking to the old guy, but cannot hear what they are saying.

"Jeez, Billy," says Meadows, "that's a lot of truck."

"Never go small, kid. Let me show you what this truck has got."

"You got Mule off okay?"

Billy gets out of the truck and assures him that Mule is safely in the bosom of a Greyhound bus and on his way back to the comfort of his parsonage and the grace of God.

They roll the coffin to the tailgate and Billy proudly demonstrates.

"Check it out," he says and brings the lift level to the coffin. Together they half-lift, half-slide it off its wagon and onto the lift.

Billy leans back against the lift and says, "Let's take a deep breath here."

"You tired?"

"No, I ain't near tired." Billy puts the closed end of a cigar into his slicer and cuts it off. He lights up. "But this is your last chance to think about what we're doing here. You can make it a lot easier on yourself."

"You don't want to do this?"

"I didn't say that. This ain't about me."

He blows smoke rings, the first widening as the second comes behind, and the third.

"I don't want to make it easier on myself," says Meadows.

"That seems to be your thing, which I can relate to, by the way. Guys like you and me, we take discomfort till it's pain, we put up with inconvenience till it's disaster, and then we're cool, the worst has happened, like we always knew it would."

"All I know is I can't do this without you."

"I'm here. I want to do it. I got nothin' more I want to do, or need to do."

"We got to do *something*. What power do we got? They eat us, they eat our children."

Billy cocks an eye at him. "Well, this would be something, barely. This would say something, if anybody would listen." He puffs on the cigar, blows on its end to make it glow. "I just want you sure of what you're doing."

"I'm never sure of what I'm doing. It kills me."

"You married that girl . . . what was her name?"

"Mary." He utters the name wistfully. The name alone, just overheard in a crowd, someone calling for a friend, can make him cry.

"You married Mary, you were sure of that, right?"

"I was one hundred percent sure of that."

"And you had a kid, you were sure of that kid, right?"

"Sure, I was."

"See?"

Meadows turns and looks at the casket, putting his hand softly upon it.

"They sent him to a godforsaken desert because . . . who knows why? It wasn't to protect America . . . that desert couldn't do nothin' to America. And then they sent him back to me in this, with more lies, makin' a big show of what a hero he was . . . and all the honors . . . and Arlington. Was that all for me? Or is it for them? I ain't gonna bury no Marine. I gotta bury a *son*. I'm through with the Marines, and I'm through with the Navy. I'm through with all things military. I'm done with sitting in their brig, I'm done with stocking their shelves, and I'm not gonna let them use my son anymore."

Meadows puts his shoulder to the side of the casket and pushes. Billy puts his shoulder to the other end and together they push it inside.

Washington watches the truck pull away. His watch is over. He walks toward the transient barracks. Tomorrow, back to the suck.

Five

As soon as Billy crushes an empty Bud can and tosses it the length of the room, Meadows routinely retrieves it and drops it on top of the others in the plastic-lined wastebasket of the very same Howard Johnsons room they occupied the night before. Now, as then, and as the night before, dinner is pizza delivered to the door. They aren't into food. Billy is fuming. They should be in Philadelphia by now. Beyond Philly, even, on the road, tooling north in their rig. That's where they should be. Instead, they are back where they started and lucky to be alive, if that's so lucky.

"Best years of my life," says Billy.

"When?"

"Defending this country. It was who I was."

"Me too, but only for that little time. Before I fucked up. I wasn't defendin' nothin' yet. You know what I think? I think your best years are still ahead of you."

"Oh, fuck you."

"I was only tryin' to make you feel better."

"I don't want to feel better."

"Then excuse me."

"I gave it all I had. I was a good sailor."

"You were. I know that. You were an example, kind of."

"Look at me now, I got no chick, I got no child. All my future is behind me. I got a scrambled brain held together with a steel plate. And they look at me and what do they see? They see a fuckin' terrorist!"

"They don't know you."

"They don't know you neither."

"They don't know anybody."

"It used to mean something, being an American. There was a spirit, a unity, some goddamn common sense. Some well-earned pride."

"Fuck 'em. Fuck 'em all."

"I concur, goddammit."

Billy pops another can of Bud, sucks some of the lukewarm beer down. The air has been poisoned by those assholes and must be neutralized. It is more than having their trip so rudely derailed; a sense of what is right has been perverted; a tradition of how people should be treated has been broken. He has had a lifetime of snafus and disappointments: of liberties cancelled and shit details drawn, of good duty denied and bad duty imposed, of decent officers transferred and assholes assigned in their places, of women who signed off as soon as he shipped out, but this goes beyond the bitches of circumstance.

Here is what happened: With the first roll of the wheels of their rented truck the road trip began with exhilaration, in spite of their sad mission, the kind of inner joy that comes from snubbing authority without a fallback plan, from doing something stupid on the face of it but correct at the core. And it wasn't just Billy. Meadows seemed more himself, reminding Billy of that time they got him his cherry popped, or that time Meadows stood up to a waiter and made him take back the cheeseburger and make sure the cheese got melted this time. Then, just about when they might have laughed at themselves, they encountered the roadblock at the gate, armed troops lined against them.

Meadows freaked and yelled to stop the truck. Billy thought, oh, I'll stop the truck, right up their ass is where I'll stop the truck. He wanted to punch it, mow them down, an impulse less than rational but there it was and what was he going to do with it? It would be the end, of course, but not a half-bad way to go, and quick enough. A blessed end to his flowing and ebbing pains, from the top of his head to the soles of his feet, an end to nights of broken sleep and unsettling dreams of strolling main decks with twenty-year-old girls in their summer dresses, of wanting to fuck and not being capable of it. What did he have to lose? That bar, which O'Toole was probably looting and which at the end of every month was a headache of paperwork? His foot, at first taken off the gas, went back on it, in defiance of the handheld bullhorn ordering them to stop or die. Then he realized he wasn't alone in this and he hit the brakes.

"A fuckin' apology would have been nice," says Billy.

"I heard someone say he was sorry."

"Sorry they didn't smoke our asses."

And there it was again, on the TV, the bald corpsman, his latexed hands shining a light into Saddam's open mouth, securing the perimeter, and afterwards the dictator tugging on his own wild beard and leaning back with a puff of captured resignation.

"There's your terrorist," says Meadows.

"Or not. Nobody found a bomb on him neither."

"We have to start all over again," Meadows says, then thinks for a minute, "or else they really did kill us and we're in hell now. We'll show up at the hangar tomorrow and go through the same thing, over and over again. Why would God put me in hell?"

"And why would He put me in it with you?"

They manage a chuckle. Billy sucks down the dregs of the Bud and tosses another empty across the room. Meadows picks it up and drops it into the wastebasket.

"Will you sit the fuck down?"

"I'm nervous."

"You're makin' *me* nervous."

Someone knocks on the door. Billy looks at Meadows, his eyes narrowing, if that's possible, considering how narrow they have been.

"Should I open it?" he whispers.

"I could care less," Billy whispers back.

Meadows goes to the door and opens it.

Mule comes in out of the chilly night air, and drops his bag on the floor. He stands facing Billy down, as though Billy has much to answer for.

Billy vacates the bed he is on, which he has rumpled in his discontent. Mule looks at him and at the bed with a certain distaste. Billy moves around the bed, smoothing it out, like an eager housemaid in training. He pulls the bedspread back and turns down the top, fluffs the pillows.

Mule sits on the side of the bed, pulls up his failing legs, and lies down in his overcoat.

"Hi, Mule," says Meadows. "I thought you went home."

Mule says nothing. He needs another moment.

"Did you miss your bus?" asks Meadows.

"I called my wife from the police station. The police station. Only after they decided I was not a Muslim radical, not a threat, and not a mullah."

"Was she upset?" Meadows asks, worried. He really likes Mule's wife.

"Oh, she wanted me to come right home. But I told her that when times demand it even old men should become threats. If all you can do is stand with two canes, where they can see you, why, then that's what you do. If all you can do is sit in their way, then you sit in their way. The students did it last time, maybe this time it falls to the old men . . . and women. I told her—"

"The fuckers are turning their own good people into enemies, goddammit! It's like when they thought everybody was a communist. If you don't do what they do and say what they say, you're a fuckin' communist, the enemy."

"I believe I was talking," Mule says icily.

"I'm sorry, your holiness," Billy says. "What were you saying?"

"I told her that I was not coming home."

"You can always go home again," says Billy without irony.

"We come close to getting shot," says Meadows. "And then they had dogs sniffin' my boy's casket."

"They could have settled it all with a phone call or two, or some polite conversation," says Mule, "but, no, they let their paranoia consume them. You can't expect decent people to stand by and take it."

"So we start again tomorrow?" asks Billy. "One more escort detail."

"Fuckin' A," says the man of God.

* * *

In the morning, when they go down for breakfast, they are met in the lobby by the Marine light colonel. This time they catch his name, Willits. The lance corporal, Washington, is with him. The motel staff is used to seeing military men in uniform, but even they seem interested in this meeting between unlikely civilians and the Marines.

"What's this deal?" says Billy.

"Good morning, gentlemen," says Colonel Willits. "I've been briefed on last night's snafu."

"I got your snafu," says Billy.

"Everybody's touchy, and nobody more than those in the new level of bureaucracy. Apparently, you rented a truck, a Ryder truck, which nowadays, as you know, is a symbol of . . . something or other."

"A bomb, I guess."

"A big bomb, yes."

"Hell, make it a dirty bomb, no extra charge."

"If you think about it, all bombs are dirty," says Meadows. "I never heard of a clean one."

"Anyway . . . the rental agent apparently went off the deep end."

"That cunt."

"Billy," says Mule, "if you can't let the man talk, at least make your interruptions less profane, please."

Billy does an overstated roll of the head, a man awakening in an alternative universe.

"It was a case of hearing things that weren't said, seeing things that weren't there. Totally ridiculous, but there it is and what's done is done," says the colonel.

"And you're here for, like, what?" says Billy.

"Excuse me, but it might be more productive if I knew who I was talking to. Are you the honcho of this little patrol? Or should I be talking to the father of the Marine in question?"

"I got a mouth, I use it," says Billy.

"Too often, some would say." This from Mule.

Billy shoots him a look. How about a little support here?

Washington, behind his stoic face and next to his rotting earlobe, is having a good time.

"Sir?" the colonel addresses himself to Meadows.

Says Meadows, "My heart is broken."

The others fall silent for a moment, as though just now realizing, yes, that's what would happen.

"Billy's the honcho," he says, "just like before. Talk to him."

"Very well, then." Colonel Willits turns to Billy. "The offer of interment at Arlington National Cemetery is still open. Arlington is a resting place that should not be refused lightly. There lie heroes. I don't know why the details of the Lance Corporal's death were embellished to make it appear more heroic than it was, but mark this: his death was heroic. He was in a foreign and hostile land doing a decent thing. I didn't put him there and I can't question the CiC's reasons for putting him there. But he was there as a Marine and he served with honor and he died a hero. He deserves to lie beneath the sacred soil of Arlington, and I believe that if he could make the choice that is what he would choose. So . . . you're the honcho," says the colonel, staring down Billy, "what do you choose for him?"

If possible, Billy hates him even more now. Break out the bugles, fly the flags, play out the ritual in the garden of stone, chalk up one more dead hero and let's all go home. What's a gesture, after all, but a pain in the ass to the one who makes it and a fading memory to anyone who might notice it?

"Back up just a little, Colonel," says Billy. "You tellin' me you can't question the commander in chief's reasons for sending this man's son to his death? You don't know how? Or you never thought about it?"

"A Marine is willing to die on order. In fact, he is already dead."

Billy does another head shake, stranger in a strange land. "Maybe I've been a fuckin' civilian too long," he admits. "Washington, you already dead?"

Washington does not answer. Perhaps he hasn't thought about it. Or he has thought about it too long.

"There has to be a reason," says Mule.

"No, Reverend, just the order," replies the colonel.

"But the Marine might have a father and a mother, and they have to have a reason, or how can they live with themselves? They all were told there was a danger to our lives, an imminent danger. Huge arsenals of horrible weapons, aimed at us," says Mule.

"The Marines, on the other hand, were told, there's the mission, go do it. We did it. Mission accomplished," the colonel says.

"That's my point, what mission? Destroy the arsenals that weren't there?"

Billy says, "And if the mission was changed and declared accomplished, why the fuck was Meadows's kid killed?"

"Mopping up," says the colonel. "Sometimes it's the worst part."

"He was delivering fuckin' *school supplies!*" says Billy.

Meadows listens but says nothing.

"You have to have a reason," says Mule. "For the parents, and for the rest of us. Just say it: I'm avenging my father's disgrace. We need the oil. God told me to. Something. Just so it's believed."

"I don't engage in political discussions," says the colonel.

"Is that what we're havin'?" asks Billy. "Because we don't know shit about politics. We're just ordinary dudes. All we know is, you have to tell the fathers and the mothers something, and it might as well be the truth. It's too late once you go in and bomb the country to say, we had to free the Iraqi people from a mad dictator. That might have worked, if it was said in the beginning and if it was true. Mothers and fathers might have thought that was worth their children's lives. Me, I wouldn't have. I would have left the Iraqi people to figure it out for themselves, the way other oppressed people have. And then if they ask for help you either give it to them or you don't. But at least there would have been a *reason*. Only I would of wondered, why Iraq and why not North Korea? Why not Iran? Why not a dozen other places in this fucked up world? Even so, at least it would have been on *principle*. I could have been won over."

"I can't speak to all of that," says the Colonel.

"No, I guess you fuckin' well can't," says Billy, "because if you could, maybe it wouldn't be happening." He looks to Meadows and cocks one eyebrow. Mule waits for the response. Finally, Meadows looks down and shakes his head. "Colonel Willits?" says Billy. "Thanks, but no thanks. Me and my friends are gonna take Larry Junior home and bury him in New Hampshire."

"And not in his uniform neither," says Meadows. "I'm gonna bury him in his graduation suit. If it still fits."

* * *

The colonel is unruffled. Offended, to be sure, but otherwise unaffected. He has no control over the emotions of civilians. In a free society, some benefits cannot be imposed upon those unwilling to receive them. This thing is done, on to the next thing. He asks if he might buy them breakfast.

"You got somethin' more to sell, Colonel?" asks Billy.

"Good will, and it's free."

They take a table at the Howard Johnson's. Washington is not used to eating with colonels or civilians. The waitress has to ask him to repeat his order and when it comes he doesn't pounce on it as you might expect a Marine to do. He moves the chow around on his plate, watches the others and eats when they do.

"You could rent another truck," says the colonel, "but there are disadvantages to that, not the least of which is it's a long drive."

"And some assholes might shoot at us," says Billy.

"Your government would like to put the casket on a plane," says the colonel, "and fly it right to Portsmouth, deliver it to a funeral parlor of your choice. I might be able to get you three on the same plane."

"My government would be willing to do that?" says Mule, thinly sarcastic.

"Yes, Reverend, it would be an honor."

"Tell me, is it true that your CiC hasn't attended a single funeral or memorial for any of the war dead?"

The colonel's spine stiffens. "That cannot be true."

"Well, it is true. And he's the only war president who never did." Billy is impressed. This old Bible thumper knows more than the Psalms.

"I expect he will, though," says Meadows. "Before next November."

They can't help it: the two old sailors laugh.

The colonel says, "I suppose he doesn't want to impose on families in their time of grief."

"I suppose he's already imposed on them by sending their children to die," says Mule.

Says Billy, "You got us steamed now. We're angry old men and we're making a gesture."

"You're cutting off your nose to spite your face."

"Take a look at this face. Does it give a shit?"

"Look, I understand. At least some of it. But I'm not the enemy here. How can I help?"

"Come with us. You can do the heavy lifting."

The Marine colonel finds that amusing. No, that he could not arrange, even if he wanted to, which he does not.

"Let's go by train," said Meadows, "like we did before."

"Before?" asks the colonel.

"When you were the chasers? And Mr. Meadows was the . . . ?" Washington starts to say, then stops himself.

"Was the what, Lance Corporal? When Mr. Meadows was the what?"

"The prisoner, sir."

The colonel looks at the two old men and the aging man with new interest.

"I did eight years in the brig. I came out with a DD," says Meadows.

The colonel can't mask it in his eyes. There is nothing lower in all of military life than a Dishonorable Discharge. Here he is trying to do the right thing by a coward with practically no rights of citizenship left. His impulse is to walk away from the table, but he still has in his possession and under his direct authority a dead Marine and a Silver Star candidate. And an unfinished picture.

"That's quite a serious court-martial," says the colonel.

"I was eighteen. I stole forty dollars from a polio contribution box in the base PX."

The colonel knits his brow. Were things so different then?

"I had some problems."

"They fucked over the kid because the Old Man's wife was in charge of the polio drive," says Billy. "It was her project, you know how it goes. So the Old Man had to make a gesture. Now it's our turn."

"They don't even do that anymore," says Meadows. "Polio drives."

"And you two?" asks the colonel. "How do you figure into it?"

"First-class POs in transit," says Mule. "We drew the chaser detail."

"And out of this a relationship formed? A lifelong . . . what? . . . friendship?"

"Apparently," says Mule.

"Fuckin' A," says Billy. "Why not? Life ain't that long."

"The Navy," says the colonel, shaking his head in wonder and disdain.

"What about it?" Billy bristles.

"Shore Patrol should never be temporary duty. You can't ask ordinary sailors to be cops."

"You ask ordinary kids to be killers."

"We train them to be killers from day one, and that's a permanent designation, mister. That's their job description. They don't make friends with the enemy."

"Then why are they delivering school supplies?" asks Billy.

"I wouldn't give that order," replies the colonel.

"There were Marines in the brig with me, this was during 'Nam," Meadows says in reminiscence. "Marines who refused to go over there. They were all gettin' BCDs, Bad Conduct Discharges. Only they called them Better Career Decisions. Because at least they were gonna stay in one piece. They called my DD, Da Dope, like it was a good thing. Who knows, maybe it was. Maybe it saved my life. They were mostly black guys."

Mule does not mention his own BCD.

* * *

By the last bite of syrup-soaked pancake on Billy's plate, he accepts the colonel's offer to clear the way with Amtrak, to settle any necessary paperwork, bypass any legal restrictions, and to arrange for a local undertaker in New Hampshire to meet their train.

"All right, Colonel, I'm gonna let you do that much for us. Me, I'd just as soon get me a U-Haul this time, but the kid wants to take the train."

"I like trains," says Meadows.

"So do we all, kid, so do we all, another part of American life we kinda miss. We'll take the train and we'll take your word, Colonel, that you're not trying to fuck with us."

"Then we're done here." He takes out a cell phone and punches some numbers. "I'll have all the arrangements made before we get back to the base. One thing, though. Lance Corporal Washington here has to go with you." He barks into the phone: "Colonel Willits here. You are going to make a few things happen, ASAP."

"Hold on, Colonel, we don't need no trained killers babysitting us."

Billy chuckles to himself. He's kicked ass on any number of "trained killers," drunk and sober. They sell their own image better than they buy it back. Billy looks at Washington and wonders if he's hurt the young Marine's feelings, like he cares. Like Marines have any feelings.

"Stand by," the colonel tells whoever is on the other end of his phone call. He holds the phone against his chest, below the medals, and says to Billy, "I wasn't implying you need protection or that you couldn't handle it without help. Washington's on TDY, escort duty. You don't want him, he goes right back to Baghdad."

"Let's give the kid a break," says Mule.

"Does he pull per diem?" asks Billy.

"Of course." The colonel turns to Meadows. "And he was your son's best friend."

"Can't he come, Billy?" asks Meadows.

"You want a Marine along?"

"He's not just a Marine. He's Larry's friend."

"You want to come with?" Billy asks Washington.

"I go where I'm ordered, sir."

"I didn't ask you that. I asked you what you wanted. You want to come with?"

Washington nods, one eye on the colonel.

"Okay, but he takes his orders from us."

"He takes his orders from me," says the colonel. "But he will accommodate you in any way you ask. Because I just ordered him to."

"Well, you're a fuckin' force of nature, ain't you? It would have been fun to run into you in my younger days."

"You think so?"

"One of us woulda died and one of us woulda gone to the brig."

The colonel gets back on the phone, issuing more orders.

They leave Billy's Taurus at the motel and ride with the Marines in their carryall, back to the hangar where the casket has been taken. They see more flag-draped aluminum coffins being wheeled into the hangar, six of them this time.

Their casket is loaded onto another carryall. Washington will go with that one. As the first carryall with the civilians pulls away, Billy turns back to see Washington standing at attention beside the other vehicle and the colonel in his face. He wonders what that is all about.

"The Lance Corporal is still ours," the colonel is saying with some intensity to Washington, their noses only inches apart. "I don't give a fuck what they say. The Lance Corporal is a Marine until he goes into the ground, and he remains a Marine for the period he is under the ground, plus a hundred years. I will not have two senile civilians and a DD brig bird pissing on my Corps. Is that understood?"

"Yes, sir!"

"Your mission is to provide cover for the Lance Corporal and to protect the sanctity of that dead Marine, to see that he is buried with dignity, goddammit. Is *that* understood?"

"Yes, sir!"

"The Lance Corporal gets buried with honors, befitting a Marine. Nothing less."

"Yes, sir!"

"In his uniform, not in some pussy civilian graduation suit!"

"Yes, sir!"

Washington barks his affirmatives like a good Marine, but the orders ring less threatening now. They used to be scary in their ferocity.

"And don't let that Billy Bad-Ass dude outflank you. He's old, but he's dangerous. You let down your guard, he will put you in a world of hurt. Don't let that happen. Kill him first."

"Sir?"

"That is not an order, by the way."

"Yes, sir."

"And just because that preacher reminds you of your father is no reason to trust him. He's dangerous too."

"I never trusted my father, sir."

"Good man."

"I never knew my father, sir."

"Lance Corporal, if you got a personal problem, go see the chaplain. Do you copy the mission?"

"Yes, sir!"

"Then get on it."

Washington snaps off a salute and gets into the carryall. As it pulls away he turns back to the remains of his best friend and says, "It was *my* turn to get the Cokes. The *fuck,* Larry."

"What?" says the E-3 airman driver.

"Nothin'. Just get us to the train station."

* * *

At the station, under cloudy skies, the three old sailors watch the aluminum casket with the flag banded over it being loaded into a cargo car on the train they will take to Wilmington. Lance

Corporal Washington stands at attention and salutes as station handlers put it aboard. Then he gets into the cargo car with it.

Billy looks at the sheaf of tickets in his hand and says, "Full circle."

"What?" asks Mule.

"From Dover, Delaware, to Dover, New Hampshire."

"That's real close to Portsmouth," says Meadows.

"A hearse is gonna pick us up at Dover."

"We're already in Dover."

"The other Dover."

"Oh."

Billy offers Mule his arm and Mule takes it. They get on board the train.

"What's our first stop?" asks Meadows, as they find their seats.

"Wilmington. It's only thirty-five minutes. Then we gotta change trains to Philly."

Billy and Meadows sit next to each other, facing Mule, who takes his Bible from his AWOL bag and opens it. He looks up from his Bible to see Billy studying him. "What are you looking at?"

"When did you become so old?"

"I think it happened over the past thirty-four years. Same as you."

"I categorically deny it."

"You can deny it all you want to, categorically or otherwise. That ain't gonna stop the clock or turn it back."

The train lurches forward and they are off. Meadows smiles. "Here we go again," he says.

"What's the word I'm lookin' for, Mule?"

"You know full well the word you're looking for. You know more words than you let on."

"Déjà vu."

"That's the word."

"Only this time people aren't staring at us."

"Were people staring at us?" Meadows asks. "Back then?"

"Oh, yeah. Two Shore Patrol with sidearms and a prisoner in handcuffs. That was drama."

"This isn't comedy," says Mule.

"I remember a class of school kids, on a field trip through the train station. They all had little boards hanging around their necks with their names on 'em. One little girl was name Desirée. Who'd put a name like that on a kid? Sounds like a Creole whore. The kids pointed at us. I think we scared them."

"I don't remember any kids," says Mule.

"Me neither," says Meadows.

"Least of all some little girl named Desirée."

"I'm surprised I do. Most times I don't remember shit. It's the déjà vu kickin' in."

The train starts picking up speed.

"Where do you figure little Desirée is now?" muses Billy. "Hittin' the big four-oh, a couple husbands behind her, a big behind behind her . . . a bratty daughter goin' out with sailors, a son smokin' reefer, a shit job at Burger King . . ."

"Not all life turns sour," observes Mule.

"Maybe that's the difference between running a church and running a bar," says Meadows.

"Speaking of which, I gotta check up on that fucker O'Toole, see if I'm still in business."

"I think Desirée was a cheerleader in high school and the Homecoming Queen," says Meadows, his head back, seeing it all play out on the overhead. "She married her high school sweetheart, Bo, who was the quarterback. Bo's dad owned the local Ford dealership, and for a while she worked there too, in the finance office, fixing people up with their car payments when they bought a new Mustang, until she had the twins and became a full-time mom. Right now, they're in the process of livin' happily ever after."

"Why not?" says Billy. "I'll go along with the gag."

"Thank you," says Meadows.

Billy gets up and says, "I gotta go take a piss."

"Don't try to escape," says Meadows, laughing.

At first Billy doesn't get it, then he remembers the young fucked-up Meadows shoving Mule and elbowing Billy hard enough to deck him. This was between the cars, on the way to the club car, after the disastrous side trip to visit Meadows's lush of a mother and realizing that any small dream of the future was gone now, gone before he was ever sentenced. Mule grabbed him by the jumper before he could open the door and fetched him a good one to the midsection, putting an end to that little attempt at suicide or escape, escape in either case. And then the two of them shouting the facts of life into Larry's face: next time they shoot him; do your time; live it day by day and wait for the world to change. They tried to be hard, but the kid was so soft their hardness disappeared in him. He had no friends but them, and they were willing. They would do this as friends.

And here they are the thirty-odd years after, friends again, taking a fucked-up kid to Portsmouth, this time with no chance of escape. Dead is dead.

* * *

They have a quick lunch at the Wilmington station. Billy and Mule eat like old men. Chicken and rice soup. Tuna salad sandwich. Billy has to eat through the side of his mouth, cautious of an implanted front tooth that carries no guarantee; this one goes and it's a bridge for him. For Meadows, however, it's still a cheeseburger, fries, and a chocolate malt, in spite of a cholesterol count hovering around 262.

"How long to Philly?" Meadows asks.

"Less than half an hour."

"I feel funny leaving Larry Junior with Washington."

"He wanted it that way."

"He shouldn't have to eat alone, though."

"He's not alone."

After lunch they still have some time before boarding the new train to Philadelphia. Billy wants to call O'Toole and see if his bar is still standing, but the only public phone still operational is in use. Billy berates Mule for not owning a wireless phone, and because it's been a while since he's berated him for anything.

"I'm sure young Washington has a cell phone," says Mule.

"Why would he have a phone? He's a *Marine*."

"Because he's young."

Billy thinks it's unlikely but they might as well check, they're going that way anyway.

Washington has just finished his sandwich and coffee, sitting on a stool in the baggage car, the coffin on the floor nearby. An attendant is in the car with him. Washington has told the attendant who they are and where they are going and why.

"On that Arlington thing?" says the attendant to Meadows. "I don't blame you, if I may say so."

"Well, it's just . . . we decided to do it our way."

"You're the father, are you?"

"Yes, I am."

"Hell of a thing."

"Yes, it is."

"They're running out of room in Arlington. Used to be any vet could have himself buried there. Now you got to have either a Silver Star or a Purple Heart."

"They wanted to give Larry a Silver Star. They can keep it."

"Oh, if you're killed in combat, you qualify, no problem there. But I don't think it's the same, not since Clinton started selling spaces to his pals."

"Get out."

"Well, not selling exactly, but giving waivers to his big political contributors, fat cats who never served a day of military duty. That makes the hallowed ground more like hollow ground."

"I hear you," says Mule. "You're a vet?"

"Yeah. I was there in the Gulf War, first time around, and thank God I'm not pissin' blood and my babies are okay. That was a filthy little war, but it was a righteous war. You can't let the big ragheads swallow up the little ones. I qualify for a national cemetery, but when I die you can cremate me and throw my ashes off the Horseshoe Curve up in Altoona."

"Well, I hope that won't be for a long time," says Mule.

"Could be today," says the attendant. "Anyway, we'll take good care of your boy back here, don't you worry."

"Thank you," says Meadows.

"Hey, Washington, you got a wireless phone?" Billy asks the marine.

"No, sir."

"See?" Billy taunts Mule. "I knew he wouldn't."

"I got one," says the attendant. "Here, call anywhere you want to."

"Thanks, bud. What's your name?"

"John Redman."

"Well, I'm Billy Bad-Ass, and I appreciate the use of the equipment. How do you use it?"

"Just punch in the numbers like you would on any other phone and then press 'Talk.'"

Billy dials up his bar. The attendant whispers to Washington, "Is that really his name?"

"It used to be, back in the Navy," says Mule.

"Oh, okay, yeah," says the attendant, as though that explained it.

Billy has O'Toole on the phone, asking him how it's going . . . any problems . . . should be back tomorrow or the next day . . . you able to handle it? While Billy talks, Meadows invites Washington to come sit with them in the coach. Washington says maybe later. Then Billy's tone changes.

"She said what? . . . This was when? . . . Just today? . . . I don't believe this shit. What did you say? . . . Yeah . . . yeah . . . All right, you gave me the message. . . . What am I supposed to do? . . . Listen up, just run the joint if you can. If you can't, lock the fucker up. If anybody comes in there asking anything, you just dummy up."

"What was that all about?" asks Mule.

"You ain't gonna believe this."

He hands the phone back to John Redman, who presses the button to end the call.

"O'Toole had a call from Janet down at the neighborhood bookstore where I shop. She was lookin' for me."

"You buy books?" asks Meadows.

"Once in a while, 'cause TV sucks and you got to do something sittin' there all alone. Anyway, they called her. The fuckers called her and wanted to know if I ever bought books at her store and what books did I buy."

"What fuckers are these?" asks Meadows.

"The Home-fuckin'-land Security fuckers! They want to know what books I'm reading!"

"What books are you reading?" asks Mule.

"Some of this, some of that, nothin' in particular."

"Anything that might raise a red flag for paranoids?"

"John le Carré? I read his new one. But he's a fuckin' Englishman, who cares what he says? Michael Moore. I read his latest. Dude can't write for shit and he thinks he's funnier than he really is, but when he's right he's right. I read a book called *Jarhead* by a whiny Marine, a trained sniper who never had to fire a shot but's all fuckin' war weary. Once in a while I buy a copy of *Mother Jones*. 'Fuck's the difference? The assholes have no right knowing what I read."

"Looks like somebody gave them the right," says Mule.

"Well, it wasn't me, and I figure if it wasn't me, they don't have it."

"Calm down."

"Next they'll want to know what movies I see."

"I don't even go to movies anymore," says Meadows.

"Me neither," says Billy. "Unless this gal friend drags me to one."

"I just rent a video."

"I suppose they can check on those too," says Mule.

"They'll want to know about my gal friend, who I hang out with. The fuckers'll check out my bar!"

"It's probably nothing, just SOP to follow up on any incident," says Mule.

"What incident? Us? Renting a Ryder? They were wrong, they admitted it."

"Yes, but they're probably directed to follow through and do something else, like snoop into your reading habits and your email."

"I don't got no fuckin' email. Now I know why."

"They're probably checking out me too," says Mule, "and I do have email, with parishioners. Some of that is pretty private stuff."

"Not anymore, shipmate. And, kid, I wouldn't be surprised to find out you're out of a job when you get back. You're a fuckin' terrorist, Navy ain't gonna let you in their PX."

"Good. I don't want their goddamn job," says Meadows.

"It's the only job you ever had, what are you gonna do?"

"There's shelves all over, coast to coast, north to south, full of stuff. There's Walmart, there's Target. I'm sick of stockin' shelves anyway. There doesn't seem much point in it."

* * *

The Philadelphia-bound train pulls away. They are less than an hour from Newark, where Mule hopes to call his wife and find out if anyone has called the library, which is where Mule finds his reading material. He is too poor to afford to buy books. They settle in for the ride. Meadows looks at the shabby industrial sights going past the window. Mule once again opens his Bible and once again is struck by its aptness: God selecting a burial site for Moses, in Deuteronomy. "He buried him in Moab, in the valley opposite Beth Peor, but to this day no one knows where his grave is." What a comfort is Christ the Lord. With that and one's own integrity, and a bit of food and drink, a man has all he needs. Surely his Muslim brothers feel the same way about Mohammad, and they must struggle as he does to quell the same seething anger in the face of corrupt and greedy men who use these precious objects of devotion to lubricate their own fanatical machinations. He cringes every time he hears a politician intone, "God bless America." It is fake, it is hollow, with no more truth or meaning than the shout of young Meadows's killer, "God is great." God will bless good deeds, not false posturing. For His own greatness, He needs no sycophants.

Billy says, "You ever get your dog?" He is talking to Meadows.

Billy and Mule sit next to each other now, riding backwards. Meadows sits facing them and whatever comes their way outside the window.

"What dog?"

"You always wanted a dog, was blue you never had one. Would of settled for a cat, you said, but you never had one of them neither."

"Well, yeah. I got a dog. I've had a dog ever since I got out of the brig. Not the same one, 'cause they don't live that long. Different ones. But I've never been without a dog, mutts that I rescued from the shelter. Sometimes I had two at the same time. Got an old black dog now, named Swiper. My landlord's watchin' him for me while I'm gone. He likes him too. How come you asked me that?"

"Just rememberin' stuff."

They were bumming around New York, trying to draw out the trip, trying to have some kind of good time before putting Meadows on the shelf. The visit to his mother in Camden, and her rummy boyfriend, turned out to be a big mistake, but Billy was still hoping they could do something. They'd been drinking beer, somewhere in Chelsea maybe, because they were walking down toward the Village, and Meadows had to go and say he never even had a fuckin' dog. What did this kid ever have in life? How could he have so little, lose what he had, and have everything else go so wrong? And still going that way. Losing a wife and a son in the same year. Okay, cancer, what are you going to do, but losing a boy in Iraq? For reasons that the crowd in power will have to make up as time goes by, all the buzz words that mean so much to us but are so confusing to the ragheads: freedom, democracy, oh, look, a constitution. No dog, Billy said, no fuckin' dog, we're on a train here, we're going to prison. Of course, no one said anything about actually getting a dog. Meadows, with a few beers in him, was doing what every drunk does, wallowing in his own regrets. Then he said even a cat would be nice. Billy was going nuts, because if he could have he would have bought the kid a dog and a cat and a pomegranate tree. And Mule had to open up his mouth and say, a little turtle would be nice. Of course, Mule was drunk too and just being stupid. Look at him now. A nappy gray head with two canes, glasses sliding down his nose, reading that Bible like a road map. How do I get out of here and to the Promised Land? Save me from promises. What am I doing here? What do I care who gets buried where, including myself? Where it says "Person to notify in case of emergency," Billy always writes, county coroner. Was he so bored behind the bar that he leapt at the first distraction? He must admit he felt a lift seeing Meadows show up, knowing after all these years that he was whole again, at least in one piece. Alive at least. Like seeing again the son you thought you might have had, were rumored to have had, an event Billy half-hoped for, a young man showing up—young? he'd have to be forty-plus; even the women he chases after are younger than that—and claiming his patrimony, which Billy would gladly give him. He'd rather pass on his business to a long-lost son than have one of O'Toole's friends torch it for the insurance.

"What about that kid Washington?" Billy says.

"What about him?"

"I don't know, he doesn't say much, him and his Baghdad boil."

"Well, that's because he's back there in the baggage car."

"Yes, for all we know he may be in deep discussions with the attendant, what's his name?"

"John Redman. Hell, now that guy is forthcoming. We know more about him than we do about Washington."

"What do you want to know about him?" asks Mule.

"I don't want to know nuthin' about him," says Billy.

"Sounded to me like he is an individual heavy on your mind."

"I was just wonderin'. Nothin' heavy about it."

"Go back and talk to him, if he's such a mystery to you."

"Everything's a mystery to me, except you."

"Seek and it shall be revealed."

"Preachers ain't that hard to figure. They all got the same mother."

"A son of a bitch is still a son," observes Mule.

"So where does that leave a motherfucker?" says Billy. Meadows laughs, but he is not sure he is supposed to.

"You have an audience of one," says Mule, "but for some comedians that is enough."

"I think I will go back and talk to Washington."

"I'm sure he'll enjoy that."

"Ask him if he wants to come up here and sit with us," says Meadows.

Truth is, Mule is just another dude he doesn't know anymore. Why should he? It was only those four days, five, and then the time they went AWOL, when they were so pissed off at themselves and each other they wouldn't even drink together. Can thirty years really change anybody? The essentials were already in place. Billy would have bet the farm they were two sides of the same coin, or else why would he even be here now? True, he didn't want to be, it was his wife made him come—and what about her?—cobbler cooker, church organist, soul of decency and reason, what's Mule doing with a woman like that? Billy could never be with a woman like that, she wouldn't let him. Mule did give it up early, he was going home, he was on the bus, he'd had enough. Now here he is, showing a little of the old fire at least, but articulating to Billy as though he were beyond redemption, which he damn well might be and who gives a flying fuck? Oh, there were many times on different ships he saw the God thing coming, but not in Mule. He saw it in other dudes, like "Ditty" Baggs, the yeoman, who wouldn't let you cuss around him, who prayed, and had long conversations with God, like Republicans do. You see things coming in certain shipmates: who's going to wind up sucking a cock someday, like Wowak the quartermaster; or who's going to die young, like Malloy, the bosun. Somehow you see it coming. Talking about lifers here, not your basic four-year hitch and out. Why waste time thinking about short-timers? Those others, though, the lifers, somehow you see it coming. When it happens, it doesn't surprise you. But he never saw Mule winding up as a saver of souls, talking down his nose, articulating.

He stops in the restroom for a couple quick tokes. He takes a joint out of his cigar case, and furtively sucks a little high out of it. He realizes how lucky he was not to have had his stash discovered during his terrorism bust. Those goons would have loved to ruin what was left of his life for three measly joints. It's amazing what otherwise rational people will do to prevent others from finding small pleasures in their own lives, in their own ways. Not the goons, who probably are no longer rational, but the great masses of otherwise decent people who believe the war on drugs is a real thing and a benefit to society. People are so ready to believe in anything once it is called a war. Call it a war and you'll get their support: a war on poverty, a war on illiteracy, a war on indecency, a war on crime. All fake. War itself is fake.

He pinches off the joint and puts it back into the cigar case. He waves his hands through the air in the cubicle and ducks out again, moving quickly toward the end of the train.

When the kid had his first toke, he was there too. Maybe his last, to look at him. Kid was always scared to death of getting into trouble, all the good it did him. Trouble just seems to descend on that kid. Kid? What is he, early fifties? Fifty-one, fifty-two, but still a dumb, scared kid. Sweet and innocent, still. That was in New York, when they ran into Billy's ex-wife after chanting with the Buddhists or kids who were looking for something and

Buddhism appearing to be it, and her inviting them to crash in her little apartment in Soho, where Meadows immediately fell in love and suffered sexual fantasies about her, which led to their next adventure: getting the kid laid. And Billy himself, when they left two days later, questioning whether the Navy was worth it, music to Charlotte's ears, even though she didn't believe it, wouldn't till she saw it, which she never did because he never had a chance to show her, having in the meantime got his skull fractured and kind of losing it for an extended period of time, at the end of which he could not bring himself to follow through on a deeply felt impulse, that is, getting together with her again, because Lord knows, in spite of her New York City pretensions, she was the best fuck he ever had and he never should have taken that so lightly, because if the fucking is extraordinarily fine you've already gone a long way toward making everything else pretty good. Marrying her was not a mistake, leaving her was the mistake, not that he had a choice, in his mind. He was in the Navy, goddammit, and nine months away was just another deployment, without email, without telephone calls, with only snail mail and that sporadic at best. Well, it couldn't hold. A lot of new Navy marriages couldn't hold, and their vessels became floating heartbreak hotels. The loss was in the name of duty. It was all that meant anything to him in those days. Duty, the one clear hard nail on which he could hang everything. He wasn't learning a trade. He was a signalman. He wasn't preparing for a career on the outside. He was a lifer. He was the backbone of the US military. Kennedy was blockading Cuba, ordering Billy to face down advancing Soviet ships bearing missiles, and if necessary kick ass. Fidel and Che were trying to push past their Russian sponsors to get their trigger fingers on the button that could start a nuclear war and take the revolution global. It would have been a Naval war, that one, and the thought of dying in it did not rattle Billy one bit. Charlotte and he would hold hands, two-handed, her on top of him, and they would rock, down to her back, down to his back, back and forth, joined cock to cunt, until they came and collapsed together. Why would a man leave all that for the cruel sea? Where is she now? Is she even alive? She could be a grandmother by now. Does she still rock the boat? Would she? Could he? Sometimes Viagra doesn't work, and when it does it calls for advance planning, and what he loved most about Charlotte was it came out of nowhere with her. Ever ready, a lot of times ahead of him. You didn't have to ask. You didn't have to find a proper setting. God, he misses that and the special way her skin felt against his, then, because now, all these years later, the skin on either side probably wouldn't feel so hot; still, he wouldn't mind trying it. He never expected to see Meadows again, who's to say he won't see her again. He could get Meadows to find her on the Internet. Meadows, he also remembers, stole some little thing from her apartment and confessed as soon as they were back on the train. It was a recorder or a piccolo or a sweet potato, something that made music. Mule and he just cracked up over it, but the kid was bereft. He wanted Billy to call her and plead his case. Billy promised he would, he'd take the rap, he told the kid, but then he faked the phone call because he couldn't trust himself to talk to Charlotte again. He had to sort it all out and see her on the return trip, after they delivered Meadows and he and Mule would go their separate ways. The kid stole other shit too, along the way, candy bars and little things, and it cracked them up at first, but later they saw it was indeed a sickness, a thing he couldn't help, which only made the sentence he was going to have to serve so much harder to be a part of and still call yourself a man.

Billy knocks on the locked door of the baggage car and John Redman opens it.

"It's the Bad-Ass!" says Redman. "Come on in, see how the other half lives."

Washington is still sitting on his stool, facing the casket of his fallen friend.

"Hey, how's it goin' back here?"

"Fine, sir."

"Would you like a cup of coffee?" Redman asks Billy.

"No, thanks."

"Old Navy man, you don't want coffee?"

"It's not me, it's my prostate. My fuckin' body's turnin' on me."

Washington has already turned away and looks at the floor. Billy senses that maybe things are beginning to pile up on him. It can't be healthy sitting in a closed car like this with the dead body of your best friend.

"TDY can be a bitch," Billy says.

"I don't mind."

"No, 'course not, he was a friend."

"My best friend."

"You didn't hang with the brothers?"

Washington looks up at him. "There's no rule," he says.

"Just seems to work out that way. Unless things are different now."

"I liked the dude. I liked hangin' with him. He had my back, and I had his. He was honest, said what he thought and what he meant. He was simple, in a good way. You could count on him. He never put on a face."

"Sounds a lot like his father."

"Except for the honest part."

Billy feels an urge to smack the kid, and he wonders where that's coming from. He doesn't have to defend Meadows or anybody else. That's the beauty of it.

"Meadows is not a dishonest man."

"He stole stuff. He even stole from charity. That's pretty cold. Cold enough to get him eight years in the brig."

"I know things you don't know."

"Yes, sir."

"The time you get in the brig don't say it all about the offense. There's always someone with a hard-on."

John Redman nods his head, he's seen that happen, but he stays out of this.

"And some things you can't help yourself. Doesn't excuse it, but it does make it different. Meadows was an honest kid, in all the things that matter. It's a damn shame his son never knew that."

"Yes, sir, I guess it is."

"Where you from?"

"I told you. Oakland."

"I forgot. What else did you tell me?"

"About Larry and how he bought it."

"Yeah, I remember that. I won't soon forget that."

"Me neither. It should have been me."

"It coulda been anybody. But it was that dude right there." Billy nods toward the casket.

"Either way, it's all changed now."

"Why don't you come up and sit with us for a while, see some scenery. John Redman will look after things."

"No problem," says Redman.

"That's all right," says Washington. "I'll sit here with Larry."

"No, you have to get out of here for a while."

"Why?"

"You have to talk to Larry's father, say something nice."

"I don't know what I can say that's nice."

"You'll come up with something. He needs that now."

"Yes, sir," says Washington, rising to his feet. He follows Billy from car to car until they reach their seats. Billy sits down next to Meadows, Washington next to Mule.

The train is already pulling into Philadelphia, under still cloudy skies. The people outside are bundled up against the cold. Billy wishes it would snow.

The platform is not crowded. Most of the people waiting for the train are carrying shopping bags.

"Christmas shoppers," Billy observes. "Probably going back to Trenton with their treasures. Not too busy, considering it's so close to Christmas."

"It's still early in the day," says Mule. "A lot of people will stay and have a nice long lunch in the city."

"I bet there's lots of good places to eat in Philly," says Meadows. "Philly cheesesteak sandwiches."

"You do your Christmas shopping yet, Washington?" asks Billy.

"No, sir."

"Me neither. The spirit hasn't moved me yet. That's what it's all about, Christmas, shopping for stuff and then worrying you got the right thing."

Mule won't take the bait. Not that Billy doesn't believe that that is exactly what Christmas is about, what everything is about: buying and selling.

"The important thing is," he goes on, "that the store sells more shit this year than they did last year. Sell one percent less shit and Christmas is a bust. Oh, my God, we did worse than last year! What's the matter with people, don't they believe in Christmas? It's the war against Christmas!"

"Are they gonna let you go home for Christmas?" Meadows asks Washington.

"No, sir. I go right back, after this."

"I always had the duty over Christmas," says Billy. "I didn't mind. I volunteered. Let the married men go home. I always took New Year's Eve. Took the liberty bus to New York, went nuts."

"It's a shame," says Mule. "You're already here, you'd think they could give you a break."

"This is a break," says Washington. "Sorry, sir," he apologizes to Meadows. "I didn't mean it that way."

"That's all right."

"Rough over there, huh?"

"I'd rather fight the terrorists over there than in our own backyard," says the Marine.

Billy hears the echo. All during Vietnam: better we fight communism over there than in our own backyard. Recycled sentiment keeps the machine rolling.

"Maybe," says Billy, "that was the strategy all along. Fuck a whole bunch of weapons of mass destruction."

"Sir?"

"They wanted to draw all the terrorists into one country. Get 'em all concentrated somewhere, and what better place than Iraq? Did they expect them to fight? Terrorists don't fight, they murder. They all ran out of Afghanistan, but Iraq was made to order for them, a gift. So they all ran there. Might be a cool move, let 'em blow up Iraqis, they won't be blowin' up us."

"That's just plain silly," says Mule.

"When you stop believin' what your own government says, you start believin' almost anything."

"Who's supplying them, is the thing," says Meadows. "A thousand pounds of explosives has got to be expensive and it's got to be big. A terrorist has to buy it somewhere with money he gets from somewhere else, and then he has to carry it somewhere."

"Everybody knows where the money comes from. Saudi Arabia. To keep them from terrorizing *them*. But the gang won't touch Saudi Arabia."

"Why not?"

"Friends of the family. They're all oilmen, after all. So they've made us think the Saudis are our allies. We got the Hummers, but they got the oil."

"You mean they *aren't* our allies?" asks Meadows.

"With friends like that . . ." says Billy.

"So where does that put Washington here?" asks Mule.

"Today, Baghdad, tomorrow, who knows? Yesterday it was the communists, today it's the Muslims, tomorrow it might be the gays. Who knows? There's always gonna be some threat to the American way of life, buddy. It's built in."

"Man, when did you become so cynical?" asks Mule.

"I guess it was that day we dropped Meadows at the Portsmouth brig."

They look at him and realize he isn't joking.

"Well," says Mule, "in spite of everything, I believe in this country. I believe it is a land of opportunity and freedom. And there's enough to eat."

"I never said otherwise. But when honesty flies out the window, cynicism flies in."

"It might be time for a lube job on that plate you got in your head," says Mule.

"You don't fuck with my plate, it's pickin' up WOR, New York."

They laugh and Washington relaxes. Their talk was putting him on edge. It's not easy being a trained killer sitting in a train like anyone else.

"So really," Billy says to him, "what's life like for the basic grunt over there?"

"It's all right," says Washington. "We got burgers and fries and onion rings all night. And there's a new a Burger King and a shopping mall out at the airport. We're livin' pretty good for a combat zone. Only they don't like us there."

"We gotta be the only army expects people to like us. Nobody's gonna like us," says Billy.

"When you go out," says Washington, "you never know what's gonna happen. But it was that way at home too."

"He's from Oakland," offers Billy.

"I'm used to people dying unexpectedly. My brother was only ten. Drive-by. A stray bullet. My older sister too, same way. My father was robbed on the street and they put one in him, but this was long after he had left the family so I didn't much care about that. I didn't even know who he was until they killed him."

"Jesus, kid . . ."

"I'm only sayin' . . ." says Washington, but he doesn't go on to say what he is only saying. That it's no big deal? That violence has colored his childhood and now his youth as much as anything else: school, girls, games? More.

"So you joined the Marines," says Billy, "to get away from all the killin'."

"No, sir, I was looking for a personal forge. I wanted to strengthen my character."

Sounds like recruiter talk to Billy, the kind of shit a four-point-oh recruiter lays on a doofus high school senior with acne.

"That's the way it was with Larry too. That's why we partnered up. We felt the same way about things."

"When Larry was little," says Meadows, "he played with toy soldiers. He dug trenches for them. He put them through basic training. And then, when he was fifteen, sixteen, he'd try to hang out with 'Nam vets and hear their stories."

"Yes, sir, I knew that. He wanted to experience adversity and hardships, to forge himself into the man he wanted to become."

The forge again, thinks Billy. He thinks it might have been in one of their ads on television.

"He hated Iraq, but it's where he wanted to be," Washington says.

Billy is still thinking about the forge. The GI, the volunteer, doesn't give a shit about politics. He's in it for the forge. Somebody's going to have to replace these wars every generation with something as meaningful to young men, and now women. Like, what?

"He must have been embarrassed," says Meadows, looking at the floor, ashamed of himself, "knowing his father sat out the last years of the war in the brig for . . . for a stupid, stupid reason. I woulda gone over there to Vietnam, if I coulda. I wish I had. I wish I was killed over there."

Déjà vu all over again. The kid's coming unglued. He's going to be bouncing off the bulkheads soon, makin' his way to the door, throwing himself to the tracks, and this time Mule is too slow to catch him and Billy too old to deck him. Billy makes eye contact with Mule. We got to get off this train, walk him around a little. Mule's eyes don't say yes, don't say no.

The exchange of passengers in Philadelphia occurs quickly and without confusion. Everyone seems to know where he's going. The doors shut and the train is under way again, bound for Trenton, Newark, and New York City.

"Mr. Meadows . . ." says Washington. "Larry wasn't embarrassed or ashamed of you. He loved you. What made Larry different from most of the grunts in our squad? He had a happy childhood."

"He said that?" His head is up now, his face brightens.

"Yes, sir. He had a mother and father who loved each other and loved him. He knew that and cherished that. He had a nice house to live in and plenty of good food to eat. He did good in school, played basketball. He had nice friends and he stayed out of trouble. Not everybody gets all that."

"It's a rental, but it's a nice little house. We share a driveway with the landlord," says Meadows dreamily. Billy can see he is back with his little family in his little house.

"All I ever had," says the young Marine, "was a shit job at Walmart and disrespect, but I was gonna make the most of that. I was gonna work hard and do my best till something better came along, but nothing better did come along and they cut back at Walmart and my job was gone and nobody cared but me. Now I'm employed. I got a good job. With combat pay I make a little north of twenty grand a year, plus the bennies. I got room and board, medical and dental. Financially, it's a good deal."

When Billy was an E-3, he made eighty dollars a month. He never thought about money, only duty.

They sit in silence for a few minutes. Washington looks up from the floor to Meadows's face.

"Mr. Meadows, it was my turn to get the Cokes. That was my bullet, not your son's, not Larry's. I was gonna go, but he jumped out ahead of me, said, no big deal. Wouldn't even take my money. He fucked up, Mr. Meadows. He fucked it up bad."

Oh, shit, thinks Billy. What's a father supposed to do with that? And what's the kid after, forgiveness? For what? For living? Just when he was saying something nice, too.

Meadows doesn't give him forgiveness or anything else. He is lost in another moment at another place.

"A gray car pulled up to the house . . ." Meadows starts, and he looks out the window, as though he sees the car coming into the driveway.

Billy knows it's still the nice little rental, but the wife, love of his life, the somewhat slow Mary, is gone, gone for the better part of a year, and it is just Meadows at home, doing whatever Meadows does when he is in the quiet house.

"I thought it was somebody visiting the landlord. I looked out the window. Then I saw the government plates and I knew. I knew, but I couldn't let myself believe it. First Mary, and now . . . I opened the door before they could ring the bell. A Marine lieutenant and a Navy LCDR chaplain. The chaplain stood with his hands folded at his belt buckle, that shiny brass buckle. 'Mr. Meadows. Mr. Lawrence Meadows?' I nodded. I couldn't open up my mouth. 'The Secretary of the Navy has asked me to express his deep regret that your son was killed in action.' Killed in action. Nothing about murdered while buying Cokes for the guys. Nothing about killed while trying to get the Baghdad school system up and running." Meadows looks away from the window, at the three riding with him. "Let me tell you something, the school system in New Hampshire *sucks*. Mary was developmentally shorted and *she* was smarter than most of those New Hampshire high schoolers. So I have a question."

Billy thinks he knows what it is. They wait for it.

"Why wasn't Larry back in New Hampshire delivering stuff to our own shit schools?"

Nobody says anything.

"Is that a stupid question?" asks the bereaved father.

Six

New Jersey passes below their wheels, outside of their windows.

"Yo, Jersey boy," says Billy. "Don't go jumpin' ship on us."

Billy is trying to kid him, but it may not be the right thing to say. They've been quiet for too long. In Billy's darkest imagination he can easily see Meadows jumping off the train. Go a little darker, he can see himself jumping off the same train.

"I haven't seen New Jersey since I was here with you guys."

"No shit?"

"Never came back again."

"That was a bad day, that day," says Mule. "That was a bad idea, that idea."

"It was an okay idea," says Billy, since it was his. Both Meadows and Washington have sunk down into themselves, and Mule has been lost in the Old Testament. What they need is a short sea story, a little disaster rendered comedic. Lift the spirits a click.

"What idea was that, sir?" asks Washington, playing into his hand.

"We were taking Mr. Meadows here to prison," says Billy "He was eighteen, E-l, busted, down and out. It was winter, like now, only colder. It was freezing out. Our teeth were chattering. He tells us his mother lives in Camden, right along the way, so I thought, eight years is a long time, why not let the kid say good-bye to his mom? Is that such a terrible idea?"

"We didn't know his mom," says Mule.

"She wasn't . . ." says Meadows to Washington, looking for the right words, ". . . a very responsible mother."

"I have a good mother," says Washington. "I can say that."

"It's good you can," says Mule.

"Oh, my mother had her good points, don't get me wrong," says Meadows. "But stopping by to see her, well, it just didn't work out so hot."

"It was a disaster," says Mule.

"She was shacked up with a low-life," says Billy.

"I hated that man," says Meadows.

"So Meadows," says Mule, "is rapidly going downhill, and he was on a steep decline already, so we had to get off the train in New York and air him out a little. We walked half the town, trying to get the bad taste out of our mouths. And to resuscitate Meadows, who was metaphorically drowning."

"I got your metaphors—dangling," says Billy, and, lo, he raises a smile on Mule's face! "Stick to the story!"

Meadows laughs. Mothers come and go, but trash talking endures forever.

"Wait a minute," says Washington. "You were on the beach and you had SP armbands . . . and a prisoner in irons?"

"Not irons. Just the cuffs, and we'd scuttled them long before," says Mule.

"But we had the SP armbands on, big and bright. We were the fuckin' law," laughs Billy

"And .45s?"

"Big hunkin' .45s," says Mule. "Weighed like a full-term baby."

"Which is why we stowed them too, in a locker at Port Authority," says Billy.

"You stowed your sidearms?" says Washington, in utter disbelief.

"The fuck we gonna do with 'em?" poses Billy. "We threw in the SP armbands too!"

Even Washington laughs. "You were both bad-asses," he says.

"Jesus had not yet entered my life," says Mule. "I yielded to bad impulses."

Billy is cracking up. "Yielded? You smoked 'em out! If there was a stray bad impulse bobbin' around, you were gonna rescue it."

Mule fights a smile. "Everything seems funny years later, but it was a serious dereliction of duty, pure and simple."

"I got your dir'liction swinging, you old coot!"

"All right, all right, enough of that talk."

"So what did you do?" asks Washington. "Where did you go?"

The two old sailors and the former brig bird tell him, each from his own perspective, of their two days in the city, much of which was spent eating sausages from street vendors and drinking large quantities of beer. They laugh and fill in gaps from each other's memories, but none of them remembers, or admits to remembering, or wants to remember, that in the end it was impossible to escape the inevitability of what they had to do: hand over an unformed, fucked-up, sad-assed kid to the jarheads at Portsmouth brig. The sense of that, however, the actual feeling was so long in the past and now consummated, so to speak, by the completion of Meadows's sentence, that it does not color the sea story, which Washington is enjoying so much he wishes Larry could hear it.

For the moment, they are having as good a time as they can have.

"And then we got back on the train and headed for Boston," says Billy.

"Where Meadows is wracked with the guilts because he stole this thing out of Charlotte's apartment, the woman he is now in luv-v-v-v with," says Mule as Meadows squirms.

"It was a shepherd's pipe, hand-carved," says Meadows.

"Is that what it was?" says Billy. "I thought it was a piccolo. Let's call it a piccolo. Anyway, nothing will do but I gotta call up Charlotte and confess the crime."

"I had a problem in those days," says Meadows. "I couldn't help from stealing small shit. That was the first time I ever smoked weed. And the last time."

Billy makes a mental note to share a joint with Meadows, if he can get him away from Mule long enough.

"Two Shore Patrol and a prisoner, smoking weed?" Washington wants to ascertain.

"We had issued ourselves a short liberty pass," says Mule. "The weed was the girl's."

"Anyway, I call Charlotte and she says consider the piccolo a gift, and Meadows is on cloud nine. He has sinned and been forgiven, been rewarded, in fact, so now he confesses to impure thoughts. About my ex, if you please. We find out he's a cherry, so we decide in Boston we have to get him laid."

"And now you got your sidearms back on, right?" asks Washington.

"Of course, till we get to Boston and get a room, where we dump them again."

"I don't know what it was," says Mule, "neither one of us liked carrying that .45."

"It was an unwelcome burden, brother. I didn't join the Navy to lug a weapon around."

Washington laughs. He can picture it. You're encouraged to fall in love with your piece and for a while you do, but then, like a lot of romances, you come to hate the fucking thing and the weight of it and the smell of it and the noise that it makes when it goes off. Larry wasn't the first Marine to leave his piece behind on a short errand, like going for a shit. Only what happens is sometimes you die. Not that you don't die when you have it with you, too.

"So we all agree, not the least of us Meadows, that it's time to get him laid. How old were you when you got your first, Washington?"

"Twelve."

"My point exactly. I rest my case. Meadows here was eighteen. It was time."

"No, it wasn't. The right time was when I met Mary."

"I think twelve is way too early," says Mule.

"Don't wreck my story. Believe me, corporal, he was ready. We killed the afternoon, then found a cabbie to take us to a local cathouse."

"At this place, you drove over a hose and a bell went off in the house and all the girls would line up," Meadows remembers.

"He picks out this cute little brunette who makes a big fuss over him and apparently shows him a real good time, but then as we're leaving she pulls me aside and says, I've been with all kinds of johns and a lot of sailors, but I never had one come into a whorehouse packing a piccolo."

"She said that?" says Meadows.

The three of them crack up.

"That's so uncool," says Washington.

"What?"

"Paying for sex. Whores and pimps and all that. It's disgusting."

"Jesus, what the hell has happened to your basic GI?"

"I got nothing against sex, I just think that some things oughtn't to be bought and sold."

"It wasn't all that bad," says Meadows, and the other two laugh. That much went well, they remember.

"I guess it's all in your experience," says Washington. "The whores I know, I don't want to be around."

"No, this was like going to a friend's house, only you got laid there," explains Meadows.

"I got friends' houses where I got laid, but I didn't have to pay," says Washington.

They all laugh again. Washington needed this. Everything happened so fast, Larry getting killed, the both of them shipping back, then the whole business in the hangar with the father and his two friends saying fuck you to Arlington, and the colonel throwing this impossible TDY at him, with no chance to sit around for a while and try to make some sense of the whole thing. Okay, Larry is dead. Shit happens. He fucked up. He's going to stay dead and I'm going to stay alive, or try to. For a time there, he didn't want to try to anymore. All he wanted to do was kill Arabs. Still does, a little.

"Did you two get laid too?" he asks them.

"Pay for it?" says Billy. "No way."

They laugh at him now.

"Besides, I had only got laid the night before, when we crashed at Charlotte's pad."

"You did not!" says Meadows.

"Yes, he did," says Mule.

"You old cocksman!" says Meadows.

"I was in my thirties."

"And she was married to you, at one time," Meadows rationalizes.

"People think it's easy fuckin' your ex-wife. It's not easy. It can be very difficult. It's really easier to find a cathouse in Boston."

"I think we've covered that ground," says Mule. "Let's put that to rest, once and for all. Washington is right. Better to drop your seed on the ground than in the belly of a whore."

"Jesus, what a sourpuss. I ain't never goin' to your church again."

"You're always welcome."

"Yeah, well, don't hold things up waiting for me. Back then, the next day, I gotta admit, I was sick of hearing about that brunette whore myself. It was all Meadows could talk about. He was quite proud of himself. He said he had a hard-on so big he couldn't bend his fingers or blink his eyes. You know, come to think of it, I really miss that, having a hard-on you can hang a towel from. My cock used to stand up and watch me shave, now it watches me tie my shoes."

Mule tries to suppress his laughter. He doesn't want to encourage him.

"So where did you go then?" asks Washington.

For a moment Billy doesn't say, and Mule doesn't help him. Finally, Meadows says, "Next day we had a little picnic in the park."

"In the winter?"

"It wasn't much of a picnic," says Billy.

"It was a nice picnic," says Meadows.

"We were just killing time. We had till 2400 and we would have killed every minute of it."

"Only Meadows made a run for it," says Mule.

"He jumped?"

"Yeah, and I brought him down," says Billy. "And messed him up a little in the process."

"I deserved it," says Meadows.

"I should have waved good-bye and watched him go."

"It would have been our asses," says Mule.

"It was anyway," says Billy.

"But up till then," says Meadows, "it wasn't so bad. We had some fun."

"Sounds like it," says Washington.

"Yeah," says Billy. "It was a riot."

Washington can see the story is over. They sit in silence for a few minutes, and then he rises from his seat. He tells them he wants to go back and sit with Larry again. No one tries to tell him he doesn't have to, or that he would be more comfortable up here in the coach.

* * *

The train pulls into the Newark station. They have half an hour layover before the train leaves for New York City's Penn Station, so Billy suggests they go get a beer.

"You two go ahead," says Mule. "I'll wait here."

"You ain't that slow," says Billy, "if you're worried about missing the train."

"I don't drink. Anymore."

"Have a cup of coffee, then. You should get up and move around. You'll form a blood clot in your legs and it'll break loose and travel through your body and go into your heart and kill you, if you don't move around every once in a while."

"Well, that sounds like a good way to go," says Mule.

"C'mon, Mule," says Meadows, "all for one, one for all."

They stand on either side of Mule and pull him to his feet.

"We're a little old to play Three Musketeers," he grumbles. "Can't understand grown men who can't do anything alone."

"Aw, shaddup. Here's your walking sticks."

They move toward the door, but Billy lets go of Mule's arm and allows Meadows to be the sole support.

"I'll go back and ask the jarhead if he wants to come with," says Billy. "We'll catch up with you in the bar."

"He'll ask the porter and the engineer," says Mule. "Let's make it a party. Well, it's no party, let me tell you."

"No, but the Marine ought to come too," says Meadows.

"Washington."

"Right, Washington. He seems like a real nice boy."

"Lots of colored people are named Washington," says Mule. "I've noticed that."

"Because George Washington had slaves, and they took his name."

"So would that be something to be proud of?" Meadows asks him.

"That's a good question, son. Let's think about that."

Billy hears none of this. He makes his way to the baggage car and finds John Redman alone and shuffling through his paperwork.

"Hi, John."

"Mr. Bad-Ass. Is the world right with you?"

"That's a long conversation, and we only got half an hour. Where's the Marine?"

"I thought he was with you."

"He probably jumped off ahead of us. I'm sure he wants a beer too."

"Wouldn't mind one myself, but I'm on duty."

Billy gets off the train and crosses the platform, seeking out the bar. He sees Meadows and Mule are settled at a table. He looks around for Washington but doesn't see him. There are more people here than in Philadelphia. He sits down at the table.

"Where's Washington?" Meadows asks.

"I was expecting to find him here. Maybe he don't drink either. He sounds like a pretty straight-laced kid. Maybe he's looking for the gedonk."

"Could be he's taking a piss," says Meadows.

"Ain't our problem, is he?" says Billy. "I was only tryin' to be social."

The barmaid comes with a coffee and two pints of beer.

"I ordered you a Yuengling's," says Meadows, "since I know you're from Pennsylvania. That okay?"

"Perfect."

Half the pint goes down before Meadows can even raise his from the table. Billy puts down the glass and scopes the bar.

"You certainly were thirsty," Mule observes.

"Huh?"

"That went down awfully fast."

"Yeah, well, I'm drinking for two, now that you've got old and boring. For three, since Washington ain't here."

He drains the second half of the pint and waves to the waitress.

"You may have a drinking problem, you know."

"I got no problem. I drink all I want."

"You may be an alcoholic. I am. I recognized that and owned up to it. That's why I drink coffee."

"I drink coffee too. Only not so much these days. Booze, though, don't bother me."

"Except sometimes in the morning, huh?" says Meadows. "Like Sunday morning."

The waitress comes by and Billy orders another Yuengling, looks at Meadows, but Meadows has hardly touched his first.

"I can halfway understand your believing you have to drink for me, but why would you have to drink for Washington?"

"I don't have to do nothin' for you, and even less for Washington. What do you make of that kid? Personal forge?"

"What do you mean?" asks Meadows.

"What kind of grunt is he? I mean, is he a lifer or does he already have a short-timer's chain made up? Is he a true trained killer or only waitin' to get out and go back to Oakland and the Walmart?"

"Doesn't look much like a killer."

"What's your concern anyway?" asks Mule.

"We told him about New Jersey, we told him about New York and Boston. We told him about Meadows's mom and my ex. We told him about the detail—"

"Not all of it," says Meadows.

"Enough of it. But here he is back from the war and all he says is Burger King and the shopping mall."

"I don't think they like to talk about it."

"Meadows is right. You don't understand it unless you're there."

"Look, this ain't 'Nam. This ain't World War II. Nobody's comin' back shell-shocked from this one. They might come back with a rotting ear and missing limbs and broken hearts, but this is business. This is big oil and Halliburton's bottom line. The dead and injured are just the cost of doing business, of setting up the new market, of *cornering* the new market, and it's a cost they let their customers pay."

"How dare you," says Mule, fuming.

"What?"

"You're sitting next to our friend, who lost his son in this war. We've got his body in the baggage car."

"Jesus . . . I'm sorry, kid. I was making a point and got carried away."

"I know my boy didn't die to liberate a country. I'm not buying that. Not buying that is what this trip is all about. So make your point."

The waitress puts down Billy's refill.

He takes a gulp, a more moderated one this time.

"I mighta forgotten my point."

"One of the effects of alcohol," says Mule.

"You were talking about Washington," prompts Meadows.

"He was talking nonsense," says Mule.

"Yeah, Washington. The killin' don't scare him. He's seen more of that back home in Oakland. But *something* is scaring him."

"He saw his best friend killed."

"Yeah. But he saw his brother and his sister and his father killed. He did what he could to get away from it. There was nothing to believe in anymore in Oakland. Is there anything left to believe in in Iraq?"

"He did say Larry believed in it. That surprised me. He said he hated it, but it was where he wanted to be."

"What do you make of that?"

"Kids. They want to be part of something."

"It doesn't have anything to do with Iraq," says Mule. "You're right, it's not like 'Nam. This one, all they see is the job. They don't see the lie. Yet."

"Yeah, because once you *see* the lie, you can't do the job."

It's time to reboard the train for the leg to New York City. Meadows pays the bar tab out of his envelope of cash.

They take their seats in the coach and right on time, 3:17, the train pulls away from the Newark station.

"I gotta go drain the dragon," says Billy. "I got a quart of beer screaming to get out."

He gets up and walks to the end of the car and into the restroom. He stands patiently at the toilet. When he comes out, instead of returning to his seat, he heads back to the baggage car. Washington is not there, and something in him knew that he would not be.

"He didn't come back?" Billy asks John Redman.

"No, I haven't seen him."

"Where's his AWOL bag?"

They look around for Washington's bag, but it's not in the car.

"Now you know why they call 'em AWOL bags," says Billy.

"He didn't."

"I think so."

"Over the hill?"

"That would be my guess."

"I ought to call somebody."

"Why?"

"Well . . . I don't know. A passenger is missing,"

"So what?"

"So what? It could be serious."

"Oh, it's serious. Going over the hill is always serious."

"Didn't seem like that kind of GI."

"Things come unhinged. I did it myself once."

"You did?"

"And nobody ratted me out."

"I wasn't going to rat him out. I just thought I should tell somebody."

"Let's give him a head start."

"How long?"

"Long as we can."

"We're less than a half an hour out of Penn Station. Let me see the rest of your ticket."

Billy hands over his ticket to John Redman, who checks it.

"Don't worry about the body here," he says. "I'll be the escort to Boston, if our young warrior has gone over the side, but Boston to Dover might be a problem. You've got to change trains and take the Downeaster out of Boston. You've got to make sure somebody's with it for the transfer."

"Yeah, all right. Listen, let me have the number off your wireless phone."

"My cell phone?"

"Just in case."

John Redman gives him the number.

It's no skin off my ass, Billy thinks, as he makes his way back to their coach. Washington was part of the deal, but he was the colonel's idea. It's not like they needed him. Seemed like a nice enough kid, for a jarhead, but he was never part of this little act of defiance and disaffection. Let him run. But where? Back to Oakland? Maybe to Canada. Nobody's running to Canada these days, not like back in the day when it was the first option, the refuge of choice, certainly one that never occurred to Billy, not even on Meadows's behalf, when it might have worked and his life could have turned out much differently. Meadows's life, that is. He could have saved the kid eight years of "Gangway—prisoner!" and he still would have landed as well as he did afterwards. There must be Walmarts and Targets and Costcos in Canada, after all. There would have been a different Mary, a Canadian girl, maybe not disabled, and a different son, a Canadian boy, a kid who played hockey instead of with toy soldiers and who wouldn't have to die in a war like American sons do, generation after generation. Billy has not yet heard of anyone deserting this war, but then there haven't been any pictures or news coverage of the bodies returning, why would there be coverage of deserters? Nor has he heard anything about the suicides, though he knows there must be some, maybe more than you'd expect. No one is saying. They're managing the press this time, embedding them, co-opting them. They're craftier this time. They want to pull this off without the general public feeling the pinch. A tidy little war of liberation and anti-terrorism, easy to sell and cheap to buy back. An opportunity for a mediocre man to go down in history as a war president. Cheerlead *that*. So Washington's gone, so what? Still, something about Washington going over the hill troubles Billy. It offends him. You don't bail out of a detail, any detail, let alone an escort detail for the body of your best friend, and seek the comfort of the nearest whore, though this is obviously projection on Billy's part since Washington doesn't even like whores. Washington may be seeking out something altogether different. Whatever it is he is seeking out, he has chosen his moment, and who is to say he isn't right?

He stops before entering their coach. Should he tell Meadows? He ducks into the restroom and coaxes more out of his reluctant bladder. Afterwards, he lingers for a couple of tokes and thinks about it.

* * *

Mule has his Bible open on his lap, but he is not reading. He is watching Meadows, whose head is in his hand as he watches the city form outside the window. How little, it seems, things change. A forlorn boy and an escort who'd rather not have the task.

"I guess he went back there to talk some more to Washington, and to John Redman," says Mule.

"Hmmm?"

"Billy. Too long gone to be relieving himself."

"Oh, yeah, probably."

"How you doin', son?"

"I'm okay. I couldn't have done this without you. Thanks."

"It's a small enough favor."

"Not to me."

"Do you have someone in Portsmouth you can talk to?"

"Like who?" asks Meadows.

"Your minister maybe?"

"I don't go to church. Sorry, Mule. I used to, once in a while, when Larry was small, with Mary, but it never felt right. I can't explain it."

Mule nods his head. "All things in their time. You might give it another try, once you get home. I think you're going to need some help and support."

"I haven't thought about that. I don't know what I'm going to do with myself now. I can't afford to retire, so I guess I'm gonna have to look for another job."

"Well, not necessarily. Just because Billy . . . damn!"

"What?"

"I forgot to call my wife when we were in Newark. I wanted to see if anybody was snooping around."

"They're not gonna hassle you. You're a clergyman."

"Anyway, nothing I can do about it. I'll call her in New York. We've got a little layover there, I believe. They did check on Billy so the odds are they will check on us."

"Was this a bad decision, Mule?"

"I can't answer that. You're doing what you feel you have to do. I'm with you on that. You have to do what you know in your heart is right."

"They used my boy as much as I should let them. More. They took enough. There's something very wrong about all of this."

"No argument there."

"I watch these guys, on TV, and I think, one of them has to come clean and say something. Somebody you can trust. Maybe Colin Powell. He's a good guy, isn't he? He's the one guy in that whole crowd who might come forward and say it was all bullshit."

"Don't hold your breath."

"Then someone like him, someone in the inner circle, someone that they can't discredit."

"Oh, they could discredit Powell, if they wanted to. They could discredit God Himself."

"It can happen. We saw it happen once before. We're old enough to remember a corrupt president resigning. That's something I can tell my grandchildren."

Mule winces, a beat ahead of Meadows, who now realizes that he won't be having any grandchildren.

Billy leaves the restroom pleasantly high. The train is grinding to a stop in Penn Station.

On the public address system: "*Arriving New York City. Penn Station. All passengers are required to disembark in New York. Please gather your belongings and leave the train quickly, but in an orderly fashion. All passengers must temporarily get off the train at this time.*"

Porters hurry through the cars, hustling people along.

Billy wonders, what the hell is this?

In the coach, Meadows is helping Mule to his feet and gathering their bags. Others push by them on their way to the exit. Some people push by Billy.

"Watch where you're goin', asshole," he says to one of them.

"*Please maintain order. Take all your personal belongings with you. Leave the train immediately.*"

Mule walks under his own power. Meadows is behind him carrying all the bags, including Billy's.

"Going places used to be a pleasant thing," says Mule. "A ride on the train used to be a nice day."

It's a bomb scare, or just as likely these days, a bomb, the genuine article.

Cops herd them on the platform and funnel them past an inspection point. Certain people are pulled out of line for closer inspection.

Billy, Mule, and Meadows find themselves standing in a crowd on Eighth Avenue, moving farther and farther downtown, away from the station. The street is noisy and confused.

"This is fuckin' nuts," says Billy.

The sky is still cloudy and it's in the mid-forties, not too cold but not all that comfortable to be out on the street with your train locked up behind you. They walk down Eighth Avenue toward 32nd Street.

"What about Larry . . . are they gonna take Larry off the train?"

"They'll let Washington stay with him, I'm sure," says Mule.

"Washington's gone," Billy says.

"Gone where?"

"Over the hill, I think."

"What?!"

"I think he took it on the arfy-darfy."

"What are you saying?" asks Meadows.

"I don't think he wants to go back to Baghdad. I think he wants to become a Canadian."

"Nobody goes to Canada anymore," says Mule.

"That's what I thought, but it might be coming back. Washington might be the first of the new wave."

They find a Blarney Stone and duck inside. It's toasty and nice inside. They sit at the bar. Mule needs a little boost to make it to the stool.

Billy orders a shot of Wild Turkey with a Yuengling's back. He ignores the grandfatherly look of disapproval Mule is giving him. Mule orders a ginger ale, and Meadows is going to have another Yuengling's, his second of the day. Usually he has only one and that one not until after work.

"Now, what's this about Washington?" asks Mule.

"He wasn't there. His bag wasn't there. Nobody saw him after Newark."

"We had a nice visit, I thought," says Meadows. "I mean, he seemed all right."

"He didn't seem like he was overly distressed, like he was coming apart," says Mule.

"I don't know, there was something in his eyes. He might have died over there too."

"What are you talking about?"

"When he saw what he saw, it might have killed him, to himself."

"So what do we do now?"

"Keep on truckin', I guess. Redman said he'd watch over your boy. Nothing we can do, or have to do, about Washington."

"He might show up in Boston," says Mule.

"Yeah," says Meadows. "Maybe he just needed a breather, a little time alone."

"He could have had that anywhere on the train," says Billy.

"He might not be gone at all. He might be there when we go back."

"Who knows? It might start snowing Lotto tickets."

"How much time do we have?" Meadows asks, worry washing over his face.

"You saw that scene. We're here for a while. They'll probably cancel the train."

"Cancel the train? What'll we do? We're on that train!"

Mule asks the bartender for the public phone. Right before the men's room.

"I have to call my wife," he says.

"See, this is a time," says Billy, "where you could use a fuckin' wireless phone. You could sit right here and dial her up and you wouldn't have to get off the stool and hobble the full length of this place and then have to stand on your feet next to the shitter just to say, I miss you, dear, I hope you still love me."

"Does anyone have a quarter?"

"You'll need more than a quarter. That's another reason."

"Just to get it started. I'll reverse the charges."

"Pay through the nose for that."

"I don't think you need a quarter anymore to get it started," says Meadows. "Here's one just in case." He gives him the coin.

Mule struggles to get off the stool. He takes a deep breath and is under way.

"I got John Redman's number, for his wireless phone," Billy tells Meadows. "I can check in with him and find out what's up."

"What a mess."

The bartender brings their drinks. Billy raises the shot glass and holds it aloft. "Smooth sailing," he says, and clinks it against

Meadows's beer mug. He knocks it back and waves to the bartender. "One more before Grandpa Moses gets back, please." He takes a swallow of beer to mellow out the bite.

"Not exactly how I thought it would go," says Meadows glumly.

"These things happen."

"Well, I don't think so. I don't think what's happened in the past few days happens all the time, including a bomb scare and a Marine gone AWOL and what all."

The bartender pours the other shot. Meadows pulls some money out of his envelope and drops it on the bar.

"Hell, we're almost there," says Billy. "What's Boston, another three, three 'n' a half hours? Four? Then a couple hours to Dover. Short hop to Portsmouth. We're practically home."

"Jeez, that sounds like a lot. And right now, we're stuck. What if it really is a bomb?"

"We'd have heard the blast by now. Naw, just some asshole wanting to stop the wheels of progress, stop the world from passin' him by."

"I wonder what Larry would have said, what he would have wanted. Maybe it wouldn't of bothered him, like it's bothering me, the way they lied, the way they tried to use him. Even if I had, you know, gone through with the whole Arlington thing? Yeah, it would have been nice, but how could I visit him. I'm never gonna go to Washington again."

"See, so there's a consideration never occurred to you."

"I'm gonna bury him next to his mother, in his graduation suit. He'd like that, wouldn't he?"

"Wouldn't you?"

"Well . . . no."

"Bad example. I wouldn't mind. My mother is buried in a beautiful spot, in Pennsylvania, overlooking a valley of farmland. It's not like we'd have to talk to each other. Though, you know, when I think about it, I kinda miss talking to her. She was a real wit."

"You take after her."

"That's what she used to say. She'd say it like it was God's way of gettin' even."

"Larry loved his mom. He'd want to be next to her. And that way I can visit them both."

"Two birds with one stone."

"Not that I'm looking for convenience."

"No, of course not, but why have a wife in New Hampshire and a son in DC."

"Virginia, actually."

"I stand corrected, but you know what I mean."

"You have to admit, it is an honor, Arlington. It's an honor to be offered it."

"Sometimes the real honor is in turning down the honor."

"I know." He takes another gulp of his beer. "But wouldn't you be honored?"

"It don't much matter to me. Drop me anywhere."

"But if you had a son."

"I don't, though."

"You don't have anybody, do you? I'm sorry. I shouldn't have said it like that."

"What, you think you're gonna hurt my feelings? Things are as they are."

"Now I don't either. It's hard, isn't it, to get used to."

"You hungry? That steam table looks pretty good."

"No, I'm good."

In a few minutes, they see Mule making his way back to them.

"How's things on the home front?" Billy asks him. He gets off his stool to give Mule another boost onto his.

"She's not aware of anything. I told her to call the librarian and see if anybody is snooping into my reading habits."

"It's embarrassing," says Billy. "To know agents are checking up on you. How far can they go with that shit, and for what? Do they want to know what I had for lunch? Even I can't remember what I had for lunch."

"You had a tuna salad sandwich," says Meadows, "on white bread, pickle on the side."

Billy knocks back the second shot and says to Mule, "Request permission to have another, sir!"

"You're an alcoholic, ain't nobody gonna tell you you can't have a drink. Someday you're gonna have to tell yourself."

"Barkeep? I'm gonna have just one more drink . . . and then I'm gonna have another."

"It would be useful to keep your wits about you."

"Don't you worry about me, padre, I always got my whips about me."

"We should call John Redman," says Meadows. "It's been time enough to straighten things out, don't you think?"

The bartender pours his drink, and Billy asks him, "Say, now, is there any place close where a man can buy a wireless phone?"

"Yeah, like, on any block."

"You're gonna buy a phone," says Mule, as though it were one more transgression to add to the list.

"It's time enough we got into the twentieth century," says Billy.

"We're past the twentieth century," Meadows points out. "We're already into the twenty-first century."

"Well, there you are. You wind up runnin' just to stay in place."

"Huh?"

"There's no arg'in' about it, we need a fuckin' phone. And you, kid, you need another beer."

* * *

Fortunately, Billy is able to hold some of the luggage, because now, leaving the Blarney Stone, Meadows has to give an arm to Mule and use the other to keep Billy upright. The skies are darkening, and the streets are filling with people going home from work. Mule is annoyed with his old comrade but more tired than put out. He hopes he will be able to sleep on the train.

Meadows himself is a little buzzed from the beer and his own tiredness. He has lost his sense of direction. Mule has to direct him toward Penn Station, but they don't get very far. Billy spots a phone store, on the other side of Eighth Avenue. He attempts to cross the street, in the middle, into traffic and sure destruction, but Meadows is able to hold him back. At the intersection, though, there is no detaining him. He will burst forth into the twenty-first century. He will have a phone. It is no longer an artsy-fartsy yuppie accoutrement; it is a necessity of modern life, not to be denied.

Mule has uneasy memories of their last journey together. Then, too, Billy made them miss trains. Some people can't wait to get where they're going; others can't bear the thought of ever arriving.

They go into the phone store. A young Asian man steps forward to assist them. Billy announces, loud enough for the other customers to hear, and as though it were an unusual request in this setting, "I want a phone."

"Yes, sir. How can I help you?"

"You can give me a phone."

With just this much conversation, the young man can see he's got a drunk to deal with, but the other two seem to have control, and he is after all on commission.

"Do you have one now?"

"Young man, if I already had one, what would I be doing coming in here and asking you for one?"

"Upgrading, sir. Most of our business is in upgrades or plan changes."

"Oh."

That had never occurred to Billy. Everybody else has been leapfrogging for God knows how long and Billy is still on his knees.

"So this is your first phone?"

"Well, the first that I can carry around with me."

"All right, well, let me show you what I've got."

"And if we could hurry . . ." says Meadows.

The clerk shows them the array of phones, and they are truly impressive. Some of them appear too tiny to talk into, let alone perform all the functions he describes, a few of which Billy can't even grasp, like text messaging. What's more, they look complicated. Billy's eyes glass over as the clerk walks him through the operation. He is beginning to have second thoughts. It's not that hard to find a public phone. They're not all filthy. He's not always without a couple of quarters.

"Here's the thing," says Billy. "I don't live around here. I live in Norfolk, Virginia."

"No problem. We can set you up with a Norfolk number."

"Really? You can do that?"

"No problem. We can do anything."

"How many minutes do I get again?"

"Five hundred. Will that be enough?"

Enough? It is inconceivable to Billy that anyone could spend five hundred minutes a month talking on any phone. As a signalman, he was used to communicating letter by letter. Brevity was SOP and beautiful in itself.

Then he learns that the phone will have to be charged for several hours before it can be used, and that is a deal breaker. Billy has to use it immediately.

"No problem," says the unflappable Asian. "We have phones charged and ready to go."

His excitement wells up again. A lifeline in his pocket.

He takes the plunge. A basic Nokia for twenty bucks, with a two-year contract. In a wide arc, he brings his Mastercard to the counter. If it is still good, he will go through with this.

The card proves sufficient, and now the clerk has to do things to activate Billy's new account, including making a phone call to the Mother Ship. As he goes about this, he tells Billy about their networking program. One can call others using the same plan and not have it count against one's five hundred minutes. Billy is a little skeptical. It sounds too good to be true.

"Well, what do you care?" asks Mule. "Who do you know that's on this plan?"

"You two fuckers!" he says. "You get phones too, right now!"

"I don't want any phone," says Mule. "Don't need one, don't want one."

"I wouldn't mind havin' one, to tell you the truth," says Meadows. "I've often thought about it."

"Done!" says Billy. "Barkeep, another phone for my shipmate here."

"So he and I can talk and there's no charge, right?" Meadows asks the clerk. "Even though he's in Norfolk and I'm in Portsmouth, New Hampshire."

The clerk assures him that is true.

Mule won't admit it, but he has had occasions in the past when a cell phone would have been a great benefit, and he's thought from time to time that his congregation should underwrite the cost of one, but he could never bring himself to suggest it to the deacons. People die suddenly, marriages fall into crisis, human calamities befall without warning, and at times like that the victims should have access to their pastor wherever he might be. And he's got grandchildren to worry about, though that would rightly be his expense and no responsibility of the congregation. Forty dollars a month is a good bit to pay, however, for the convenience. Maybe he could get them to go thirty and he could pay the ten out of his own pocket.

"C'mon, Mule," Meadows urges him. "These things have three-way calling. We can all three of us talk to each other at the same time."

"Well, we're doing that, aren't we, right now?"

"C'mon, Mule."

"What if I don't like it? Now I've got a contract for two years."

"What if you fall down?" says Billy. "And you're in a ditch, and you can't get up, and nobody can see you, and it starts to rain, and the ditch fills up with water? Looks like you're gonna drown. Farewell, old Reverend Mule. But you take out your wireless phone and call for help!"

"9-1-1 calls do not count against your minutes," the clerk mentions.

Somehow Mule can envision it, and it all makes sense.

It takes a little longer than they thought it would, but at the end of it all three of them have little turquoise Nokias.

Before they leave the store, Billy has to try it out. He dials John Redman's number and looks at the others with glee when he hears the porter's voice.

"Hey, John Redman, guess who this is!"

"Ask him about the train," says Meadows. Meadows has one of the phones that hasn't been charged yet, and he does not have John Redman's number. He doesn't know who he will call first.

"Right!" Billy puts his hand over the phone and tells the others, "He knew it was me."

"What about the train?"

"Listen up, John, I'm calling you on my new wireless phone . . . hold on . . ." He looks for his salesman, calls out, "Hey, what's my phone number?"

"It's in the display."

"What display?" Billy looks at the window of the phone and sees only the clock ticking on his call. "There's no number."

"It comes on when you turn on the phone."

So Billy turns the phone off, and then turns it on again. He writes down his own number on the palm of his hand, but in the meantime he has lost John Redman. Meadows is getting a little frustrated with him, as he is with himself. He calls the porter back again and gives him his number.

"So what's the deal?" he asks, "Did they find the bomb? No bomb. What? Oh."

"What's he saying?" Meadows asks.

Again, Billy puts his hand over the phone. He says, "No bomb. They're on their way to Boston."

"The train has left?"

"Well, that's just outstanding," says Mule. It's happened again. Billy has made them miss a train, and he cares not a bit. Would he care were he sober? Mule wonders. Probably not. Of course not.

Meadows bends his eyes to the floor.

"Did the Marine come back?" Billy asks Redman. "He didn't. So you're in charge. I know we can trust you. Yeah, you're right, I think we'll just spend the night here."

"Who's gonna spend the night where?" says Mule.

Now Billy is writing on his palm again. "Seven a.m. express . . . that's an early reveille. You got anything a little later?"

"Let me talk to him," says Mule and he wrestles the phone away from Billy.

"Everything's fine," Billy tells Meadows.

Meadows nods but not convincingly.

Mule learns that they could catch the evening train to Boston but it wouldn't put them there until midnight and they'd have to spend the night in Boston because there is no train to Dover until the morning. He hands the phone back to Billy, but Meadows snatches it away.

"Mr. Redman, this is Larry Meadows, the father?"

Meadows is concerned about his son's body, now speeding toward Boston without military escort or father by his side. After a minute he hands the phone back to Billy, who studies it for a moment before ending the call. He does, however, keep the phone on stand-by, though the only one who could possibly call him is the man he just hung up on.

* * *

They walk to a two-star hotel in Chelsea. This time separate rooms are available, but even one room comes close to emptying Meadows's brown envelope. All that remains are three singles, a five, and a handful of change. They bunk in together.

Mule eases himself down onto the rollaway, pain radiating through his legs. His head is against the wall. Meadows takes a pillow from the bed and puts it behind Mule's head. "I'm fine," says Mule.

"You looked uncomfortable," says Meadows.

Billy is already on the bed, his hand around the TV remote. He turns on the set and they see once again Saddam Hussein submitting to the corpsman's cavity search, the rustle through the wild hair. Something in the dictator's eyes reminds Billy of Washington: defiance, anger, powerlessness. He changes the channel. A basketball game. All ten players on the court happen to be black.

"Oh, look," says Billy. "A show on black history. Is it that month already?"

Mule rolls his eyes.

One of the players steals the ball, breaks away from the pack and goes airborne a step before the foul line. He flies through the air, defying gravity, and aggressively stuffs the ball into the basket.

"Let me point you out something," Billy says, professorially. "The most overrated shot in basketball is the slam dunk. What does it mean, anyway? What does it say about the guy who executes it?"

"That he's pretty tall," says Meadows.

"Guys were tall before. They didn't go around hammerin' the ball through the hoop. My opinion? It's an ugly fuckin' shot that they're stuck with now. Everybody's got to do it. Hangin' from the hoop, all that shit. Fuckin' butt ugly. Now, you take a fadeaway jump shot. A man is covered, fenced away from the basket. He goes up in the air, drops back, arcs that puppy over the opponent. That's a thing of beauty. That's elegant."

"I'd have to say the free throw," says Meadows. "Games are won or lost on free throws."

"Well, that's true, but nobody likes to watch someone shoot a free throw."

"I do."

"It interrupts the fuckin' game, and if it's free, you don't have to work for it, so it's boring. But mano a mano, a player goes up, fades back, that ball floats through the air to the hoop. That's a pleasure to the eyes and a balm to the soul. There's too many free throws anyway. You're not supposed to be banging into each other in this game. Fouls should be a shame. But, of course, there ain't no shame anywhere anymore."

"Listen to who's talking," says Mule. "Have you ever been ashamed about anything? Ever in your entire life?"

"Only once," he says.

Mule knows when, and asks no more. Neither he nor Meadows can discern what Billy is saying now. His voice slurs, and like the shot he admires so much it fades away and he is soon asleep in his clothes.

Meadows unpacks his phone and plugs it in to charge. He does the same for Mule's phone.

"Could you turn it back to the news," Mule asks.

Meadows gently pries the remote away from Billy's fingers and changes the channel.

* * *

An hour later, and Mule has dozed off as well. Meadows has turned off the TV and sits on the straight-back chair that goes with the little writing desk. He does nothing. He sits. The only sounds are hotel sounds, white noise, humming, and the occasional slam of a door falling back. So when he hears the odd electronic tones of, "Raindrops Keep Falling on My Head," he is startled and out of his chair, spinning around looking for its source.

The music is coming from Billy's chest. He is awake now and flailing about. "What the fuck . . . ?" Mule is awake too. Calmly, he says, "It's your new phone."

"The phone does that?"

"Answer it," says Meadows. "It must be John Redman."

Billy takes the phone out of his shirt pocket, fumbles with it for a moment, and finally presses the Talk button.

"Hello?"

"Good evening. Mr. William Buddusky?"

"Yeah, that's me."

"My name is Sharon, how are you this evening, sir?"

"Not all that great, frankly."

"Oh, I'm sorry to hear that. I won't keep you long. I just wanted to let you know that my manager will be in your area in the next few days and he would love to show you how to make a twelve to twenty percent return by investing in International Market Funds."

"Wait a minute. I don't even know my own fuckin' number, how the hell did you get it?"

"Excuse me?"

"This number is about two hours old and my head is splittin' from Wild Turkey and beer and you're callin' me to *sell* me something?"

"Have I called at an inconvenient time?"

Billy holds the phone aloft to Meadows. "Kid, turn this fuckin' thing off, will you?"

Billy gets out of bed, no small achievement, and splashes cold water on his face.

"That's what they do," says Mule. "Any number they can get their hands on. They don't see anything wrong with calling you at night, at home, at dinner or whatever. They'd like to have your other numbers too, like your salary and your bank account numbers and your height and weight and any other numbers that'd give them a little edge in gettin' your money before some other outfit does, 'cause a person only has so much money and there's so many corporations out there thinking it's theirs for the taking."

Billy sticks his wet head back out of the bathroom and says, "Huh?"

"I might take this phone back," Mule goes on. "Why subject yourself to it? Aren't we a free people?"

"I got a better idea," says Billy. "Why don't you use it to call in some pizza?"

It would be the third night running for ordered-in pizza.

"I'm bound up from the last one," says Mule. "I need a salad in me, or some fruit."

"Could we not hear about your digestive problems?"

"I'd hardly think that was offensive to someone like you."

"I shit like clockwork, no matter what I eat. I eat it, it turns to shit."

"You, on the other hand, are almost always offensive to someone."

Billy comes out of the bathroom looking refreshed, though he is still on an ebbing drunk.

"I'm up for hittin' the bricks," he says. "How 'bout you, kid?"

"Just for somethin' to eat, sure."

"Could you get up on your four legs and go out to the 'hood, padre? We'll get some rabbit food in you, get the old tract workin' again."

Christmas lights and decorations cheer the streets of Chelsea. Because of Mule they cannot walk far, and they don't have to. They find a coffee shop a block from the hotel. The chill has gone off the air and it feels like rain. The walk was nice. They could have gone farther even. The air sobers up Billy and he remembers walking the Village with these two the last time, thirty-four years ago, for all appearances three sailors on liberty, a spring in their step. On the town. Now they move at a much slower pace, and they've lost the imperative of having a good time. They just want to eat and tomorrow morning early catch their train and bury the boy.

By sheer dint of repetition, it has become a joke: Saddam Hussein's physical exam. It is on TV again, on the little set behind the cashier in the coffee shop. The sound is off. The three stand near it waiting to be led to a table. The image changes to the two sons of Hussein, in death poses, cleaned up for the camera.

"I lost one, he lost two," says Meadows.

"I guess he thought it was worth it," says Billy.

"It wasn't worth it. Not to me," says Meadows. "What were their names?"

"Who?"

"His sons."

"I don't know. Weird-ass Arab names. Ugow and Queasy."

Mule knows their names. "They were Uday and Qusay," he says. "Fairly easy names, actually."

"Yeah, if you're used to Leteesha and Kuamme."

"You are a racist as well as an alcoholic."

"You forgot sexist."

"That too, I'm sure."

"Fair to everybody. What did you name your kids?"

"Otis and Wilma."

"Now that's nice. A kid should always be able to spell his own name. After Otis Redding 'n' me, right?"

"You?"

"Wilma? After old Willie Bad-Ass. I'm touched, I am. If I ever have a kid, I'll name him after you. Dick. First he'll be little Dick and then he'll be big Dick."

"What if it's a girl?" asks Meadows.

"Lad, look at him," says Mule. "Even if he had any left swimmin' in him, what woman of child-bearing age is gonna lay down for him?"

"Your Wilma, if you'll make the introductions."

"I swear, I'm gonna brain you with my cane, I don't care if there's already a plate in your head. I'll put two of 'em there."

Somebody else's daughter, trying to make her way in the big city, shows them to a table and gives them menus. She tells them she will be back in a minute. Billy looks at her with a sense of longing and loss and finally fellow affection. He will leave her a good tip. He wonders if she has a tattoo and where it is and what it is and how she would weigh on his face.

They peruse their menus.

"It's got to get better now, though, don't you think?" says Meadows. "Now that they caught him and his two sons are dead." Meadows is still thinking about Hussein.

"Better for who?"

"Better for us. And better for them too. I mean, for the Iraqis."

"We'll see."

"I mean, if it doesn't stop terrorism, then what are we supposed to do?"

"Are you terrified?"

"Now?"

"No, not this minute, just generally."

"No, I guess not," says Meadows. "Were you ever?"

"Not really."

"The threat is always going to be there," says Mule.

"Most Americans are more terrified of losin' their jobs and their health insurance than they are of Muslim bombers. You say al-Qaeda, I say Alcoa."

"I only ever had the one job, so I never thought about it. Till now. It's not all that great a job and the money's no good, but it's the only job I ever had. With a DD, prospects weren't so hot when I got out. I'm over fifty now, so I guess they're even worse."

"See what I mean? Who can think of al-Qaeda when you're so worried your job will go away."

"Fuck a whole bunch of jobs," says Meadows and the other two laugh. They still both love it when he comes alive like this. Especially knowing that the job is all that he has left to lose.

Somebody else's daughter is back and ready to take their order. Mule will have his salad, and he's in luck, they have stewed prunes. Billy is still thinking, so Meadows orders a cheeseburger and a shake, and he makes a point to insist that the cheese is thoroughly melted and not just thrown on as an afterthought. Billy looks up from his menu with a pleasant sense of déjà vu. He orders liver and onions and a cup of herbal tea.

"Here's what I'd like to know," says Meadows. "Would it be worth his two daughters? He's got twin daughters, right? It's a real question. I had to answer it. Too late, but then I had to. Let him answer it. Invading that country and changing that regime, was it worth the lives of your daughters? Would you have given them up for that? Was it worth even one of them? Which one was it worth?"

"Good luck on gettin' that answered," says Billy.

"It's not a bad question," says Mule. "It might be the fundamental question for all wars."

"What's their names anyway? His daughters," asks Meadows.

"Leteesha and La Toya," says Billy.

"I got your Leteesha dangling," says Mule.

Billy almost chokes. Mule covers his mouth with his hand.

Somebody else's daughter brings Meadows his shake and coffee and tea for the other two.

"Excuse me, miss," says Meadows. "Do you happen to know the names of the twin daughters?"

"What twin daughters?"

"That guy in the White House."

"Oh . . . Laura is one of them, I think."

"No, Laura is the wife."

"Dunno, I guess. I'll ask."

"One of them drinks a lot," says Billy.

"Your kind of girl," says Mule.

"Padre, at this stage of my life it's hard to find a female who isn't my kind of girl, and I might be close to widening the net. In fact, you're lookin' better all the time."

"Be the best one you ever had," says the Reverend.

"I do likes the dark meat."

Meadows is laughing, remembering them as they used to be and so pleased to see that, really, they haven't changed all that much.

"Well, I do myself, so count yourself out," says Mule.

"Can I ask you a personal question?"

"God, Billy, you don't know any other kind. It makes you hard to be around sometimes."

"Man to man."

"Fortunately, I don't have to be around you all that much. Once every thirty-some years."

"How come you married a black woman?"

"What?!"

"Don't tell me you never had a white woman. It was the seventies. Every white woman in the country was looking for Mr. Black Right."

"And as I recall white dudes finally admitted to having an eye for black women."

"I'm crazy for the sisters myself. And they dig the Bad-Ass! Well, a couple of 'em did . . . for a while. But then I'd say somethin' stupid, and—"

"You? Say something stupid? To a black person?"

"I yam wot I yam, and that's all wot I yam. But I never married nobody, if you don't count Charlotte, and you really shouldn't count that. You did, though, you married your Ruth, and she looked like a black woman to me."

"First of all, it's none of your business."

"I know that. That's why I asked you if I could ask you."

"All right, then, I'll answer you. God told me to."

"To marry a black woman 'stead of a white one?"

"To marry Ruth."

"He told you?"

"Yes."

"Like he told the Reverend Pat Robertson who was gonna win the election?"

"Pat Robertson is a fraud. Anyone with the brains of a rag doll knows that."

"How come God never talks to me?"

"He doesn't talk to Pat Robertson neither."

"But he does talk to you?"

"I didn't say that. I said he told me to marry Ruth and be a decent man and stay with her forever. He didn't talk to me, not in words. He touched my heart."

"Maybe it was Ruth who touched your heart," says Meadows.

"Oh, it was, God through Ruth."

"Because that's what happened when I met Mary."

Billy wishes he had never brought it up. It is starting to make him a little blue.

"You have that feeling that something tremendous is happening," Meadows says, "bigger than the both of you, more powerful than chemistry."

"That is it exactly. The voice of God."

Bluer and bluer.

"He doesn't have to touch my heart," says Billy. "He could just pat me on the shoulder or shake my hand. If it came with a nice black girl with a cute ass, so much the better."

"I was down and out," says Mule, "and didn't care about nothin'. A recovering alcoholic with bad knees and a BCD. And, oh, yeah, I was black. Then one day I found Jesus."

"Where?"

"The only place you can find Him—in your heart. I went down in there like it was a scary cave, which in a way it was, a dark, unexplored place. Went down there afraid and alone, came back up fearless with Jesus at my side. Next Sunday I took myself to church—"

"And there was Ruth."

"Right there, and everything came together for me. I had my life's work and all a man could ever ask for."

"Well, that's a tad more than I wanted to know," says Billy. "Praise Jesus, here comes my liver 'n' onions."

Somebody else's daughter places the orders in front of them, saying, "Nobody knows."

"Huh?"

"Nobody knows the names of the twins. Sorry."

"That's okay," says Meadows. "Thanks for asking, though."

"No problem. Enjoy your dinners."

"Doesn't matter what their names are. They're safe and alive."

"And praise Jesus for that too," says Mule.

Seven

WEDNESDAY IS WARMER. THE RAIN has warmed it up by ten degrees. They don't have to zip their jackets to the neck. It's not much rain, just a drizzle. Not enough to have to buy umbrellas from the vendors hawking them on the street or to cover themselves with clear plastic ponchos, also for sale on the street. These street vendors, so early on the job, are up to the minute in weather information and the quickly changing needs of the people who hit the street in a hurry, unprepared for the day.

The three old sailors were up at six, their Navy reveille, feeling logy, now as then. They awoke in the dark and turned on the lights to dress. Billy and Meadows quickly passed through their morning routines and surrendered the facility over to Mule, who had a problem to deal with and, congratulations, overcome.

Now out on wet Eighth Avenue, the street coming alive, the three of them walk uptown toward Penn Station. Billy holds Mule's arm and moves him along. Meadows carries the bags. They did not have time for coffee. They will have breakfast on the train, if they don't miss it. All three now have a freshly charged and operational phone in a pocket, and the odd presence of that new thing takes some getting used to, like the time Billy and Mule strapped on the .45s. No, not like that.

It is too early for Mule to call his wife. He called her last night on Billy's phone, but he did not tell her he had a phone of his own. He wanted to save that for when he actually called her on it and he could tell her she was the first to receive a call. What would she think? Too early now to call, though, because she is probably taking full advantage of sleeping alone, without his snoring or flailing.

Meadows hopes his first call won't have to be John Redman. He hopes the body of his son won't be lost somewhere in one of the many arteries of the Amtrak system. He might call his landlord and see how Swiper is doing. This is the first time they've been apart.

Their bags are searched and their IDs checked, but they still are there in time to catch the 7:00 a.m. express to Boston, and Billy has once again gone undiscovered with two joints in his cigar case.

They stand in line at the club car and, since it is crowded, they have to share the table with somebody's collegiate son. He's about nineteen, with a twist on one corner of his mouth, out of which he seems to talk, like the second banana many believe is the top banana. He has red hair. He doesn't seem inclined to say more than good morning to them. They are old to him. They are old to themselves.

While they wait for breakfast to arrive, somebody's collegiate son makes a call on his cell phone, to his girlfriend back home, it sounds like, laughing about waking her up.

"I'm on the train! I bailed on all my classes." She says something and he says, "Cool." He has a Boston accent.

People have been saying cool to things since Billy was a youngster in Pennsylvania, when his generation invented rock 'n' roll. Cool came earlier still, with jazz, before groovy and after real George. What is cool in this case is that all their friends are coming home from all their colleges and the partying will be total. When he was nineteen Billy was in boot camp, freezing his ass off in Great Lakes, Illinois, fighting through walking pneumonia so he could get basic over with and get himself on a ship. He wonders if he would have liked college. He likes to read. He likes to argue. He might have been a good student, who knows? Instead he became a signalman, and there isn't any corresponding job in civilian life. Not that he wouldn't have found something interesting in college, that's what you're supposed to do, find your career path. It's hard to imagine what he might have found, what kind of company he would have wanted to work for, what kind of career would have meant something to him, meant as much as the Navy did, as the bridge of a ship at sea once did.

The girlfriend in Boston is falling back to sleep and somebody's collegiate son is a bit self-conscious to be talking to her with three old guys sitting there saying nothing and listening to every word.

"Okay, then, go back to sleep. I'll call when I get home." He puts the phone inside his jacket.

"We got phones last night," says Meadows and shows him his. "All three of us. They all match."

"Cool," he says again, because what else can he say to something like that? He himself is too old to ask why and too young to care.

"Haven't even used mine yet, but I'm thinking about it."

The kid notices for the first time the clerical collar on Mule, which makes him unaccountably uneasy, though he is an okay Catholic himself and the black preacher is obviously not a priest anyway.

They find out his name is Sean.

"Going home for Christmas vacation?" Mule asks him.

"Yeah," he says. Then, "Yes, sir."

"Where do you go to school?"

"NYU."

"I'll bet that's a good school."

"It's okay. It's the Big Apple."

"That's the real attraction, huh?"

"Sure."

Billy sits with his arms folded across his chest, watching and listening to Mule pose his small questions, wondering why. More to the point, he wonders why he seems to have no interest in starting up a conversation with this kid. Usually he would.

Meadows, meanwhile, has powered up his new phone and is pleased to hear a dial tone. He punches in some numbers and places his first call.

"What year are you in?"

"I'm a sophomore."

Billy wonders if Mule had to go to school to get his preaching diploma. He does sound a shitload more educated than when Billy knew him. Probably not, though. Black rural churches, you most likely learn on the job, or come in saying you're a preacher and then have to prove it only by the force of your sermons. Now he's got to listen to two conversations, because Meadows has his landlord on the line, or on the air as the case has become.

"Hi, Pete, it's Larry. I'm on a train to Boston and I'm calling on my new cell phone."

Sean seems to be listening to two conversations as well. Billy saw the way he looked at Meadows earlier and he could just bet that the kid was wondering if Meadows was maybe retarded and the preacher and the other guy had something to do with taking care of him. Look at my new phone. Shit, maybe he is, him and his poor wife both. Then in that case, Sean's right, they do have something to do with taking care of him. Sean tries to answer Mule's questions and listen to Meadows's phone conversation at the same time.

"What are you majoring in?"

"Business."

"Very practical. What do you hope to do?"

"I hope to be the CEO of a Fortune 500 company someday."

Apparently, Billy's instincts have not yet entirely abandoned him. Who wants to have a conversation with a kid whose dream is to spend a lifetime devoted to the corporate bottom line? Somebody's collegiate son thinks Meadows is retarded? Billy thinks the kid is psycho. Why waste a life like that, and do so much harm in the process?

"We're not burying him in Arlington," says Meadows, into the phone, "we're burying him at home. We're bringing him with us. Me and my two friends."

"That's a grand ambition, son," says Mule.

"You gotta think big," says Sean, a future Master of the Universe.

"How's Swiper? You gettin' along? Does he miss me yet?" Meadows turns to the others and says, "This is the first time we've been apart overnight."

"Well, it's still the land of opportunity," Mule tells the kid.

What is this old fucker, being ironic?

"You've got to seize your opportunities and run with them," Mule adds, with a ladle.

Billy's a beat away from reaching over and slapping him silly, but something in Meadows's tone distracts him.

"Who came in? SPs?"

Now even Mule forgets the CEO wannabe.

"And who? Hold on." He holds the phone against his chest and says, "Some SPs and Home Security guys came to my *house*." Back on the phone, he says, "And you let them in?"

"They don't give you much choice," says the landlord, Pete.

"What did they do in there?"

"Don't worry, I stayed with 'em, all the time. They didn't tear anything up. They just looked at everything, the closets and the drawers 'n' everything."

"How long were they there?"

"About three hours."

"Three hours?!"

"Maybe longer."

"What were they doing for three hours? It's a small house."

"Most of the time they looked through your computer."

"I got personal stuff in there."

"They didn't copy anything or print anything . . . that I know of."

The others hear only Meadows's half of the conversation. They watch the lines form in his face as he listens.

Their breakfast comes. Mule starts talking to Sean about the food. Even Billy says something about train food, just to give Meadows some space.

Meadows lets his eggs go cold and an unfamiliar edge creeps into his voice before he turns off the phone and puts it away. He takes a sip of coffee, puts the eggs on his toast and makes a sandwich.

"That thing works pretty good. He coulda been in the next room."

"You going to Boston?" asks Sean. Now he's suddenly interested in them, is he? Fuck him.

"Let me ask you something, as a future executive in America," Billy says.

"I'm only taking basic econ at this point."

"Say you're the CEO of United Airlines . . . you'd like that, wouldn't you?"

"Definitely."

"So say you're the CEO of United Airlines, do you worry about crashes, hijackings, people dying?"

"Well . . . sure, I would. But it's not the first priority."

"It's not?"

"No, because it doesn't happen all that often. That's an unusual occurrence. My first priority is going to be maximizing profits."

"You learned that in basic econ."

"Right."

"Well, how often does it *have* to happen?" Billy tries to keep the edge off his own voice.

"I'm sure there's a scale or a guide for that."

"You mean, to tell you when crashes and hijacks and dead people start to seriously de-maximize your profits?"

"Yeah."

"But even then, no need to panic, right? Because if people stop flying your planes you can turn to the government for a billion or two to tide you over till you can convince them it's okay to fly United again. The government can't let airlines go out of business. That's why it's called a bailout."

"It's happened, though. Hasn't it? There have been airlines go out of business."

"You got me there. A couple have gone out of business. So there must be a limit on how far the government will go to bail out a fucked-up airline. Not United, though. They're still around, probably will be for a long time. But let's say you're the CEO. You know planes have been hijacked in the past and they're gonna be hijacked in the future, and you would not like that to happen to one of your United planes. So wouldn't you think, we ought to do more than just go through the motions, we ought to *really* make sure nobody brings a weapon on board or a bomb in their suitcase? We ought to have people who are citizens of this country doing the searching, and they ought to know what they're doing. They ought not to hate their jobs, and we ought to make sure of that by paying them more than minimum and givin' 'em a few bennies. Wouldn't that occur to you, as CEO?"

"I'm not an expert."

"No, but if you're gonna be CEO of United someday, you're gonna bring with you some of who you are right now, some of what you know is right, just from livin' as long as you have."

"You'd have to run the numbers," says somebody's collegiate son with grand ambitions. "You'd have to figure cost per mile per year to do all that you're saying and see how it stacks up against the cost of hijackings per year. If it's costing you more to prevent them than it's costing you to have them, well, you're just going to take your chances and go on having them. But all in all, there haven't been that many, have there?"

"Enough, I'd say, but then I'm not an expert neither, or even a business major. I'm just a guy who takes an airplane once in a while. A lot less than I used to, because it's not much fun and it's not all that safe."

"Oh, air travel's very safe. It's the safest travel there is."

"I've heard that."

"And it's kinda fun. I still like the train more, though."

"So do we. Let me pose another question here."

"Oh, leave the boy alone," says Mule. "He's on his Christmas break."

"What? We're havin' a business discussion. I'm goin' along with you," he says to Sean. "Why pay the dough to professional screeners when we can hire schlubs from Nigeria to go through the motions? But let's look at the planes themselves. How do we prevent a hijacker once he's on board with his gun or his knife or his box cutter?"

"Sky marshal?"

"See, that's why you're gonna make CEO someday. The government's gonna pay for the sky marshal, all your company has to do is give him a seat, and you're only gonna do that if there ain't no paying passenger for that seat. Problem is, there just ain't that many marshals to go around, so you're playing the odds game. Still, better than nothing, and cheap. But think about it, you're the CEO walking around the plane, and you're askin' yourself, how can I keep a hijacker from taking over this plane?"

Sean is imagining it, with some pleasure, because in his fantasy he is wearing a three-thousand dollar Hugo Boss suit and a twelve-grand Rolex watch. The plane looks okay to him.

Billy finally has to prompt him: "To take over the plane, you gotta get in the cockpit, right?"

"Right."

"So?"

"So you make sure nobody can open the door or knock it down."

"Bingo! One plane safe from hijackers. Now you can go take your secretary to lunch at the Sherry Netherland and afterwards sneak upstairs to cop a little matinee."

Sean likes that part too, but he sees a flaw.

"Wait a minute, what if the hijacker threatens to kill a stewardess?"

"Bye-bye stewardess."

"What about the passengers?"

"Look, worse come to worst, everybody aboard is lookin' at dying. The thing is, nobody's gonna take that plane into a building or even crash it to the ground if the pilot can keep control. And the pilot has his orders, never open the door. *Never open the door.* Land at the closest airport."

"Oh . . . so you mean, what happened on nine-eleven—"

"Didn't have to happen. Forget that we didn't know who was in our country, even though we should have. Forget that we ignored a terrorist group that had declared war on us, more than once. Forget that young Arabs were in American flight schools learning how to fly big jets without bothering to learn how to take off or land. Forget that the FBI can't find its own ass in the dark with both hands. Forget that we had a president with a hard-on for Iraq and he couldn't think of anything else. Forget that we know what the enemy looks like but we're too embarrassed to pull young Arab men out of line and make sure they're not carrying weapons. Forget all that. For the want of a good door, *that's* why it didn't have to happen."

"But back then, nobody knew."

It happened when somebody's collegiate son was still a senior in high school. It is rapidly becoming a memory of his childhood.

"The CEO knew. Didn't he ever walk through one of his own planes? If his interest was in making flying safer, he would have known. Only that's not what interests the corporation. Just like you learned in basic econ class. What interests the corporation is making money and saving money in order to make more money. We doped it out and figured a hundred dollars a door would have done it. You probably got that much in your pocket right now, enough to take care of one plane. How many planes does United have, a thousand?"

"I don't know."

"Two thousand. That would be a bill for two hundred thousand dollars. About the price of the CEO's daughter's sweet sixteen party, which he *will* charge to the company."

"That's some party."

"That's some CEO."

"Excuse me, but who are you guys?"

"We're just three old guys ridin' a train," says Billy. "We got nothin' better to do than ride trains and estimate the cost of making a cockpit door safe."

Somebody's collegiate son quickly finishes his last triangle of toast and retreats from the club car.

"Stupid little prick," Billy mutters.

"He's a kid going home for Christmas," says Mule. "What in the world do you expect from people?"

"Nothin'," says Billy. "And I'm never disappointed."

"My landlord made noises like I was gonna have to leave," says Meadows. "I been there for close to twenty years."

"Get out."

"Right, like I was gonna have to get out."

"No, I meant . . . forget it, what did he say?"

"He's a GS10, works at the depot, he was rattled havin' SPs bring government goons to the house."

"Fuckers. Turnin' friends into enemies."

"SOP," says Mule. "I'm sure it's done with now. They checked out all three of us, found out we're normal boring folks, and that'll be that."

"Yeah, except I'm not gonna have a job or a place to live."

"I can't imagine it coming to that," says Mule. "Let's deal with first things first."

"I couldn't imagine none of this shit could happen, from the last election on."

"What election?" says Mule.

* * *

Meadows is the first one off the car in Boston. Once again, he is burdened with all the bags because Billy is handling Mule. He rushes ahead of the other two, looking for a station agent.

Billy can see he's found someone. He waves to them, follow me.

In a baggage room, among unclaimed luggage and cardboard boxes, sits the flag-draped coffin on a luggage carrier. Meadows is greatly relieved. He has to sit on a box. Billy puts Mule on a box too and lets everybody take a little breather. They have plenty of time, their train doesn't leave for another hour and a half.

The agent is helpful and sympathetic. He promises that the coffin will be transferred with them to their Dover train. Meadows thanks him and asks, "Can't we sit here for a while?"

"Sure. I've got to be here with you, though, and—"

"Just for a few minutes."

"No problem."

The agent goes to a far corner of the room and pretends to be examining boxes, but he is just getting out of the way.

Billy doesn't feel like sitting. He leans back against the wall and like the other two looks at the flag-draped coffin. Billy once knew all about flags. They were his life and he revered them. He particularly liked the notched Alpha and Bravo . . . the bold India and Lima . . . He could identify in an instant the flying flag of all the services, the states, and most of the countries. You couldn't stump him. Putting in to Malta, he didn't have to look it up, he'd just go to the flag locker and find the white and red with the cross inset, upper pole side corner. He once won a bet on the First Navy Jack flag. Oh, the glory of flags! The flutter of flags goes into your heart and makes you stand tall. He'd salute a flag just because it was flying. But this flag, now covering the body of a son, these stars and stripes, this was truly his flag, of all the thousands. This was the flag he would have died for, as so many before him had, so many still to fall. This flag flying from the bridge on an open sea as day was ending could move him to tears. In the early wars one honored man would go into battle with no other responsibility than carrying this flag.

"Rain Drops Keep Falling on My Head." From his chest again. It's amazing, really. He takes out the phone and answers it. John Redman, the conscientious porter, is calling to see if they've reconnected with the dead Marine.

"I figured if you caught the seven express you'd be in Boston now."

"We did catch it and you're right. We're with him right now. Where are you, John?"

"Oh, I'm on my way to Baltimore."

"No sign of the other Marine?"

"I was going to ask you the same question."

"I guess he's gone."

"He'll catch hell."

"Maybe they won't find him."

"They can't find Osama bin Laden."

"Next October."

John Redman laughs. "I gotta go now. Duty calls."

"Thanks for all your help," Billy says.

"Don't mention it. Us vets got to stick together."

Billy ends the call, stows the phone.

Meadows thanks the agent again. He feels good about what he's done and the care Amtrak is taking with his son.

"Can we leave our bags here till it's time to go?"

"No problem," says the agent.

They have more than an hour. In Boston it is not drizzling, and it's warm for mid-December, in the mid-fifties, so they go outside and get some air. Billy wants to find a cozy bar, but Mule insists it is too early to start drinking. They are on the last leg of their mission and some sobriety would be a good thing.

"We passed through Boston, didn't we, before?" asks Billy, as though age has taken a toll on his memory.

"You know full well we did," says Mule.

"Just passed through, like now?"

"All right, all right," says Meadows. "This is where you got me laid for the first time, okay? What do you expect me to do?"

"Don't hit me. I'm an old man."

"We are not going to go back to that whorehouse," says Mule.

"Did I say anything about a whorehouse? I'm takin' a walk, I'm waitin' for a train. I'm only killin' time, like I got so much left I can kill it and never miss it."

"That whorehouse wouldn't be there anymore anyway," says Meadows. "God, it was thirty-four years ago."

"Some whorehouses were in business for a hundred years, like in San Francisco. They became famous."

"I doubt that one became famous," says Mule. "A bell hose on a driveway."

"I liked that touch."

"Lawn chairs on a linoleum floor, girls in swimsuits."

"I liked that touch too."

"Could be you just like whorehouses."

"I do. Is that a sin?"

"I know it's not the sign of good mental health in a senior citizen."

"I used to like them, anyway. Haven't been in one since . . . Christ, I can't remember when."

"Could you please leave Christ out of conversations like this?"

"But all the times I was, yeah, I got a boot out of whorehouses."

"She was awfully nice, that girl," Meadows remembers. "Not like a whore at all. Just like a nice working girl, doing her best to get along. Providing a service."

Billy laughs. "I wonder if she's still there."

"Still there?!" says Mule. "She'd be an old lady."

"Year or two older than me," says Meadows.

"No offense," says Mule, "but that's pretty ripe for a whore."

"She might be the boss now," says Billy. "The madam."

"That's possible," says Meadows. "She seemed pretty sharp. I'm sure she advanced in her profession."

"Still remember her, dontcha," says Billy with a leer. "You're turnin' red, you old cockhound!"

"I predict that whore's dead and the house has been razed to make room for a 7-11 or a karate studio or a Thai restaurant," says Mule.

"One way to find out," says Billy.

"Meadows, don't let him take you there. We'll miss that train."

"We'd never be able to find the place anyway," says Meadows. "Not that I'm not a little curious about it."

"I could find it," says Billy.

"A minute ago you couldn't remember ever being in Boston," says Mule, "now you're gonna be able to find a cathouse you went to once thirty-four years ago."

"Memory's a funny thing, ain't it?"

Mule insists he will have no part of it. It's irreverent, foolish, and stupid, not to mention risky for several reasons, one of which is the surety that they will once again miss their train.

"We'll just drive by," says Billy. "You're probably right, for sure it's a Mickey D's or a Starbucks by now."

"An hour ought to give us plenty of time," says Meadows. "Got nothing else to do, except hang around and think."

Mule insists he is going to go back to the station and wait for the train, but he knows that if he does, and if they miss the train, he will wind up in Dover, New Hampshire, with a body and no money or resources or clue what next to do. When they tell him, fine, you go back to the station and have a little rest, he says shit, loud enough for the driver to hear it as they all pile into a cab. Some preacher.

Billy is laughing, telling the cabbie that thirty-four years ago the three of them piled into a cab like this and for a dollar were taken to a rather interesting whorehouse by a cabbie who, as it turned out, had been an old mine-sweep sailor, so it was swabbies on parade. This cabbie, however, is a Pakistani, with no naval experience that he cares to speak about and no knowledge of whorehouses and no great familiarity with the streets of Boston. In short, a raghead, which Billy is not going to hold against him because he has impeccable manners. That dollar is gone today as soon as the taxi door is closed. The digits rack up on the meter as Billy describes the general area they're looking for, using landmarks that no longer exist. They are into the Pakistani for twenty dollars and are about to vote on aborting the recon when Billy lets out a yelp. He's found the whorehouse.

The driveway hose is gone. The shrubbery that hid most of the house has been cleared away. The house itself has been repainted a safe white with green trim. It's possible the garage has been remodeled into an extra bedroom, Billy can't say for sure. Otherwise the place hasn't changed much.

"There it is," says Billy. "I'll be go to hell."

"I'm not sure," says Meadows. "It looks like it, but . . ."

The driver waits, the motor running.

"Can you take a credit card?" Billy asks him.

"Hold on, here," says Mule. "We are not getting out of this cab."

"Well, we have to find out if it's the same place. And if it is, if they're still in business. If Meadows's first is still in action."

"I will take a credit card, yes, sir," says the driver.

"One simple question: why?" says Mule.

"Well, if you pin me down like that, what am I supposed to say?"

"We're here," says Meadows, "we might as well go have a look."

"Then keep the cab waiting. I'll sit here," says Mule.

"At these prices?" says Billy. "Okay, if you pay."

Mule gets out of the car with them and the taxi pulls away. Mule watches it go like a lifeline.

"There's no cabs out here," he observes. He checks his watch. "And our train leaves in . . . forty minutes."

"Lots of time," says Billy.

"It doesn't look like a place of business," says Meadows.

They go up to the front door and Billy knocks. They wait a moment and he knocks again. Mule wishes he had never left his little parsonage in Virginia. It is Wednesday already and he has not given a moment's thought to Sunday's sermon, not that he hasn't been gathering material.

The door is answered, fearfully and tentatively, opening just a crack. A Latina woman balances a white two-year-old on her hip. Both faces peer through the narrow opening with wide eyes, the woman with wide brown eyes, the baby with blue.

"Good morning, ma'am," says Billy. God, he has a sweet tooth for olive-skinned women. *El mundo hispanico.* Though if truth be told, he's had a bout of yellow fever too. And at times gone gaga for the sisters. He's got nothing against white women either. Lately, it's all longing.

The woman says nothing. She looks at them fearfully.

"Do you live here?" he asks her.

"No at home now," she says.

"I don't think she speaks English," says Meadows.

"No. A little only," she says.

"Por cuantos años vive aquí?" says Billy.

That Billy is suddenly speaking Spanish, or something that sounds a lot like Spanish, does not faze Meadows. Somehow he attributes to Billy all the skills he himself does not possess. Mule, however, is amazed. He forgets for a moment the folly of this particular errand and is in awe that Billy possibly can be a fool in several languages.

"No vivo aquí. Trabajo aquí. Con los niños."

"Ah, si, Lo siento. Y el jefe? Cuantos años para él?"

"No se, señor."

"What's the deal?" Meadows asks.

"Mis amigos y yo tenemos una"—he looks for the right word—"*historia* con esta casa."

She looks confused. Wrong word. The fact is Billy doesn't feel anything about this house. He doesn't know why he's dragged them here. It seems all he wants to do, as he did thirty-four years ago, is distract them from life as they know it, at this moment, the only way you can know it. He tries to frame a request to look around inside the house, see where the girls lined up, and see where the one Meadows picked led him to a crib, and where he and Mule waited for him, teasing the girls who weren't chosen. But if she's any kind of babysitter at all she will refuse and call 911. He could ask to use her phone, to call a taxi, but she should refuse that too, and besides, they all have phones now.

"Señorita, con permiso, por favor, donde puedo buscarlo un taxi?"

More trustful now, she opens the door wide enough to point down the street. "Dos cuadras y a la derecha, hay algunas tiendas y los taxis."

"Gracias por todo."

"Da nada," she says and shuts the door.

"She's the babysitter," he says. "It's not a whorehouse no more. It's just a house like any other house, with people who go to work and a Mexican girl who takes care of their children."

"Where'd you learn Spanish?"

"In bed."

They come down from the porch and walk in the direction she pointed.

"There's a taxi down here by some stores."

"Are you disappointed?" asks Meadows.

"A little," he says. "How about you?"

"Naw, I didn't expect it would still be there."

"So why did we come?" asks Mule.

"What's the difference?" says Billy. "We've been and now we're gone."

Eight

"LET'S BE FAIR," SAYS BILLY to Mule, "if you weren't so slow, we wouldn't have missed the train."

"Excuse me? I got shit for knees. I got to use two fucking canes just to stay upright. You had to go find a goddamn whorehouse, *that's* why we missed the train, just as I predicted we would."

Meadows doesn't care. They are on the train now, and Larry and their bags are with them on the same train, thanks to that nice station agent. Granted, it's six and a quarter hours later than it would have been. It's dark out now, and cold, but they are on the train, at last. He is more concerned about Mule's reversion. His old mouth is coming back, which is distressful to hear from a man of the cloth.

Mule must know what he's thinking, because he rips off the clerical collar and stuffs it into his jacket pocket.

"Let it all out, Mule, you'll feel better," says Billy, laughing at his outrage.

The train they should have been on, and would have been on, but for Billy's whorehouse curiosity, left at noon. The train they are on did not leave until 6:15, which meant while stranded back in Boston they faced a gap from lunch to dinner, a passage from day to night. Pooling their cash, they had enough for lunch at a hot dog stand and an adult and two senior tickets to a movie, a foreign film with subtitles, though they didn't know that going in. All they wanted anyway was a warm spot to sit down. Billy would have preferred a bar, but that idea met resistance, and the movie would be cheaper, considering they had hours to burn. The movie was in French and started out looking like it was about French whores, which Billy thought ironic and probably worth watching, but it quickly turned into a sensitive story about the friendship between a Muslim shopkeeper and a lonely Jewish boy. All three of them fell fast asleep.

Afterwards, they still had some time to kill so they did go to a bar, thanks to Meadows's ATM card. He was the only one of them to possess an ATM card. Billy thought it was nuts to carry around anything that someone with a gun could force you to use to get money out of a machine. Mule, in the course of his simple life, never had any use for such a thing, but he thought that about the phone too and he had already changed his mind on that score, having called Ruth twice to tell her what a miserable time he was having and how he wished he was home. She soothed his nerves and told him to soldier on, an odd choice of words.

Once on the 6:15, it occurred to Mule that in an hour and a half they would be in Dover with a coffin. What then? Meadows checked the paperwork. The mortician who was supposed to pick them up would have been there yesterday. He took out his cell phone and called him and told him their new estimated time of arrival.

Since then Mule has been trying to get Billy to admit to the blame.

"No crimes committed, no rules broke, nobody's sinned," says Billy. "So get your fuckin' panties out of their twist."

"There's a way of doing things."

"Well, this was our way."

"Your way."

"I be the honcho."

"What master-at-arms made you the honcho?"

"Natural selection."

"What's that mean?" asks Meadows.

"I'm just rattlin' old Mule's chain. Twistin' up his panties."

"Stop saying that. And don't say, I be."

"Very well, sir."

"I just don't want to take the blame for missing the train."

"You're right, it was all my fault. We missed the train, and now we're on a train. We told the Marine Corps and the president of the United States where to get off. I'm feeling pretty good about this."

"You're tanked up with Wild Turkey and beer, you're feeling pretty good about everything."

"I gotta admit, it helps."

* * *

The undertaker and his hearse are waiting for them at the station. His name is Leland. That is his first name. Leland Tor of Tor Mortuary.

"I was told there would be four of you."

"Just us," says Meadows.

"I was here yesterday for you."

"Yes, I know. There was a problem in New York, a bomb scare, and, well, we missed the train after that and just stayed over."

"I called the colonel who made the arrangements. He said something about a Marine escort."

"The Marine had other plans," says Billy.

"Other plans? How can a Marine have any other plans?"

"I think he stopped being a Marine, somewhere between Philly and Newark."

They drive by abandoned factories. The ones Meadows can't remember are recalled by the driver. All are empty shells now.

"Watch your ass, Leland," Billy tells him, "they might be gonna outsource undertakin' next."

"American morticians are the best in the world."

"So were the American factory workers. We could make anything, and it was quality stuff. That's how we won two world wars. Don't be surprised if soon somebody figures it out that it's cheaper to ship a body to Mexico and back than to have it embalmed and dressed up here."

"Never happen," says Leland.

"That's what the people who worked in these plants used to think."

"What they ought to outsource is the CEO jobs," says Leland. "Those bandits just eat money, wipe their asses with it. No CEOs anywhere in the world make half of what the ones here do."

"That'll be the day."

"No job is safe," says Mule.

"Except yours," says Billy.

"True, but that's because there's no money in it. It's not really a job anyway. It's a calling."

"What job is that?" asks Leland.

"I'm a minister. I have a little church in Virginia."

"His collar is in his pocket," says Meadows, "because he cussed a blue streak a little while back."

"He thinks God won't hear him if he don't have the collar on," says Billy.

"All right, all right, I lost control. I apologize. Only Billy can make me lose my religion."

"I just got a great idea," says Billy.

"Stand back," says Mule. "Somebody get the fire extinguisher."

"Remember Washington saying he makes twenty grand a year? How many GIs we got? A million? Why don't we outsource that work?"

"Outsource what?"

"Soldiering. There's men in India and Pakistan, and, God, all those Russian soldiers out of work. All over the world, a lot of them already trained and ready to die. Twenty thousand dollars, shit, they'll do it for ten. For five, plus free medical and dental and vision and the PX. They're already dying making our sneakers and designer clothes, let 'em die fighting our wars for us. The money we'd save! Half the fuckin' nut. We could have good schools and everyone could have medical coverage and we could have free universities, and you could get people off the streets and into homes. Not to mention the savings in American lives. And we could get rid of veterans' benefits because there'd be no veterans. Once the foreign soldier did his hitch we'd send him back home. You know every little shitass war comes up with service-related diseases quicker than the VA can deny them. We wouldn't have to pay for all that, like Washington's rotten ear. Or the social problems, like whacked-out vets comin' home and drownin' their old ladies in the bathtub, or wasting the 7-11 clerk for puttin' sprinkles on their fro-yo because they're so into the habit of killin' that they can't turn it off. All of that can go home to Calcutta. All the armless and legless and eyeless and fuckin' heartless can go home to somewhere else. Outsourcin', baby. This is one of my better ideas."

For a moment, no one seems inclined to contradict him. For the moment, it makes an odd kind of sense. Indian doctors are reading American X-rays and lab results. Indian computer geeks are answering phone calls from confused Americans seeking technical support. Maybe Indian soldiers would like to fight our wars, at a negotiated price.

Leland finally says, "But you need . . . motivation to fight. You need patriotism, a cause."

"Enemy soldiers have more in common with each other than they do with their superior officers," says Billy. "When you're in a fight, you don't think about a cause. You think about staying alive. And some of those foreign dudes are *good* at stayin' alive."

"I wouldn't want some poor boy from India or anywhere else dying in place of my son," says Meadows.

"Why not? We've always had poor American boys dying in place of rich American boys. If your boy had the money, he would have gone to NYU and bailed out on his classes close to Christmas, had a girlfriend and parties to go to and all the rest."

"He wanted to join the Marines. He believed in it."

"It was just an idea," says Billy.

The trip is too short to entertain any more of Billy's ideas. It is, he notes in this particular case, the nearly exact distance between two pees. The hearse stops in the driveway between Meadows's house and his landlord's. Billy pees on a small bush in what he thinks is Meadows' front yard, and he is correct in that. The landlord's porch light comes on. Though he's lost the cover of darkness, Billy is in no position to stop, not now when he's got a good thing going.

Meadows's black dog, Swiper, comes running out of the landlord's house, tail wagging, and jumps all over Meadows, before the dog lifts his leg and joins Billy at the bush.

The phone is ringing when they go inside the little house. Meadows turns on a light. The house is cold. It is very neat, everything in its place. There is a small fireplace in the living room, and on the far side of that, in the corner, a desk, on which the telephone rings. Meadows answers it. It is a friend of his son's, from high school, who has heard the bad news.

Billy finds the thermostat and turns it up. Meadows motions to the fireplace, then waves it away. When he hangs up the phone he starts a fire. Then the phone rings again. Another friend. Meadows has no answering machine, so it is likely they have been calling for the past few days. He tells everyone who calls that there will be only a graveside funeral, Friday morning. The phone rings throughout the evening.

They order in pizza from Domino's. Meadows has beer in the reefer. Mule calls his wife, once before they ever go into the house and again before he goes to bed, in Larry Junior's room, where a stuffed teddy bear sits on the dresser.

Billy and Meadows bunk in together, in the bed where Meadows used to sleep with his wife.

"Your landlord wasn't all that gracious," says Billy, after Meadows has turned out the light and they are lying in the darkness.

"Well, you were pissin' on his bush."

"So was the dog, and the bush was on your side, and it was an ugly fuckin' bush anyway and ought to die."

"He's a landlord. He doesn't want grown men exposin' themselves on his property."

"What's to see?"

"He's a property owner. He has to worry about the value of his property."

"I'm a property owner. I don't worry about shit."

"You're different."

"He's gonna kick you out."

"Yeah," says Meadows, "I get that feeling. He'll wait till I get Larry buried and everything. He watched Larry grow up. They got along just fine, he don't have any children of his own."

"He got property instead."

"Not all that much. Just his house and this rental. But he has a good government job."

"So what are you gonna do?"

"Haven't thought about it."

"You gonna stay here in Portsmouth?"

"I don't know. Nothing else comes to mind."

"You might want to try another place. Fresh start."

"Mary and Larry would still be here."

"You could come visit. You got close friends here?"

"Not too many. Not too close."

"You could visit them at the same time, if you wanted to."

"I guess I can pretty much do whatever I want to do." His voice is beginning to trail into sleep. Billy gives him a jab in the ribs.

"What?" He's awake again.

"You *can* do anything you wanna do, but you gotta do it, not just think about doin' it."

"I haven't been thinkin' about anything, I told you."

"Move to No'fuck."

"Norfolk?"

"You can work in my bar."

"I never worked in a bar before."

"It don't require all that much training."

"Your bar didn't seem all that busy."

"That's my fault. I let it go. It needs new blood. It could be a going concern again. I need a partner."

"A partner? I thought just an employee."

"No, I need a partner. The bar'd be half yours, and when I go, it'd be all yours."

"Billy, you don't owe me nothin'. I told you that. I owe you, for coming with me and bringin' Larry home. And for before."

"I ain't payin' off no debt. I need a partner, and I got nobody to leave that bar to. You could stay with me for a while, but then you'd have to find your own place, because I like to pursue the ladies and, frankly, you'd cramp my style."

Meadows chuckles.

"Are you thinkin' about it?" asks Billy.

"I am. I'm picturing it. It's kinda funny."

"There you go. If nothin' else, maybe it would be fun, and what's wrong with that?"

Nine

THERE IS ONLY ONE BATHROOM in the house. From one bedroom, you go a few steps down a hallway and there it is. You go another few steps and there is the second bedroom. So once again they have to wait for Mule, who seems to need a bathroom for longer than both of them combined.

They wait for him sitting over coffee in the dining nook that is part of the kitchen. Billy knows he shouldn't have the coffee, but today he doesn't give a shit. A small white TV set is on the counter, tuned to CNN. They have stopped showing Saddam and his physical examination. He's over. Maybe he will come back when they hang him. Maybe they won't hang him. For now, he's over. It's Colin Powell instead, saying, "History will ultimately judge that this was the right thing to do." Easy to say. Doesn't cost anything. Think about it later. Much later. After everybody is dead. Let history sort it out. Now it's the cheerleader, saying, "We do know that Saddam Hussein had the intent and the capabilities to cause great harm." Classic. Look in the mirror, why don't you?

After Mule is out of the bathroom and dressed, Meadows goes into his son's room and looks inside the closet. He takes out the graduation suit, a navy blue single breasted. He holds the hanger at shoulder level and brings it into the kitchen to show the others.

"It's way too small," he says. "I mean, look at it, it's too narrow. Larry bulked up in the Marines. Before that he was skinny, a tall drink of water, as they say. This is gonna be too tight on him now."

"Leland'll make it work," says Billy. "He's a professional."

"I don't want Larry to look like he's jumping out of his clothes."

Billy doesn't remind him that it's got to be a closed coffin funeral. Nobody's going to see how well the suit fits.

"Remember when we used to call it our tuxedo?" Billy muses.

"What?"

"The uniform. We called it the tuxedo, because it was as good as the best tuxedo, at a fraction of the price. It was suitable for the most formal occasion, not that I ever got invited to any formal function, or would go if I did."

"Still, it was nice to know you were always dressed for any occasion," says Mule.

"I never wore it long enough to get that feeling," says Meadows, "before they took it away from me."

"Yeah, but no one ever forgets the first time he put it on and looked at himself in it. Wow. I'm in the Navy now, and I look pretty fuckin' good."

"I remember that feeling," says Meadows.

"Larry must have looked sharp in his uniform. The Marine uniform is pretty cool, let's face it. Nothin' like ours, but pretty cool.

"Oh, yeah. He did look sharp. He was very proud."

"Pride is the thing," says Billy. "It's no sin," he says to Mule.

"No, of course not," Mule agrees. "Not that kind."

"I could bury him in his uniform, even if."

"You know, it sounds like he'd like that," says Billy. "Hell, *I'd* like that. It means you did something. You served. Fuck what the politicians and their own sons did, you served. You stood up and stepped forward. Maybe you were wrongly used, but that's not your fault. You were there. You were willing and able. You didn't weasel out of it. You didn't think it was somebody else's duty. You took it on, man, and you looked good doing it too. Why the fuck wouldn't you, you had *pride*."

"I'm gonna," says Meadows. "I'm gonna bury him in his uniform."

"Do it. Don't let the lyin' fuckers spoil everything."

* * *

At the funeral parlor, Meadows explains to Leland what he wants. Billy and Mule leave him alone and take a couple chairs in the foyer.

"You're gonna hate to see this end, aren't you?" asks Mule

"Everything ends."

"So they say, but I don't believe it, I think things kind of change their direction."

They sit in silence for a long moment. Billy studies Mule, looking at him over his folded arms. Finally, he says, "You know what I'm gonna do? I'm gonna buy you a new suit of clothes."

"Say what?"

"I'm gonna dress you for the occasion, in a new suit of clothes."

"Why?"

"Because I love you."

"I don't need a new suit of clothes. I'm already properly dressed for the occasion, it's you needs some grooming."

"Neither one of us is properly dressed. But we will be, is all I'm saying."

"The things that come into your head," says Mule. "And out of your mouth."

"The loving you thing rattled you, didn't it, old man?"

"It's very disturbing."

Double doors provide entry to the mortuary. Most people would open just one of them. Right now, however, both doors swing open because Colonel Willits displaces a lot of air. He stops and looks at the two old sailors sitting on either side of the wide foyer. This is the kind of place in which he does not like to be. First of all, it's a civilian installation.

"Where is my Marine, mister?" he barks at Billy.

Billy is unfazed. "In the box," he says. "Gettin' ready for his big day."

"I mean the live one."

"Like you said, he's your Marine, you find him."

"If you two old malcontents aided and abetted in any way in this—"

"Fuck you," says Billy calmly.

The colonel flinches. Nobody has said fuck you to him since he got the brass. To Billy, however, it seems the natural and reasonable response to a threat, and the right of every American.

"We're old and we're poor," says Billy. "What are you gonna do to us that you ain't already done?"

"There will be an investigation. It will be thorough."

"Knock yourself out. Thirty-four years ago, I had a chance to let a fucked-up kid make a run for the border and I didn't do it. This time I would have done anything. But Lance Corporal Washington didn't need any help. He gone."

Clearly, the Marine colonel would like to hit Billy. Mule as well. It's his instinct, through training and by temperament. But he is rendered impotent, by their advanced age, by their utter disregard for him, by the way they remain quietly in their chairs and look right through him.

* * *

Friday morning dawns cold, just above freezing, and the band of friends and classmates who have gathered at the gravesite are bundled in overcoats or parkas. Billy and Mule stand at attention, Mule at the head of the grave, Billy at the foot. They are dressed for the occasion, in old-style Navy dress blues, lent to them by the owner of a tailor-made uniform shop, once he found out why they wanted them. They wear them proudly. The uniforms are complete with the insignia of their ratings: First Class Signalman, First Class Gunner's Mate. They have no peacoats but wear under their jumpers the tight wool crew neck sweaters permitted in Great Lakes during the cold of winter. Mule has left his canes leaning against a folding chair. He stands at attention, unassisted.

Billy has never participated in any of the Veterans Day ceremonies, nothing in which old guys don their mothballed military jackets over ratty cardigan sweaters and shuffle along remembering what they now think of as a better time but in truth was better only because they were younger. Now look at him. Not only back in uniform but proud. Sober and erect. Looking good.

After the minister completes the service, Billy and Mule salute. It hurts Billy's shoulder but he holds the salute. Then they fold the flag. They still know how to do it. Twelve tight triangular folds. Billy used to know what each of the folds symbolized. Though he tries to remember them now in order, he cannot. Eternal life, tributes, my country right or wrong, one for womanhood, one for fathers, one for Jews, one for Christians. At the end of it the stars are uppermost. They tuck it in tightly, so that it takes on the shape of George Washington's hat. Billy carries the folded flag in two hands to Meadows. Mule holds onto his arm for support. Billy is shaking. From the cold. He holds out the flag to Meadows, who sits on his folding chair, his eyes red, his lower lip quivering.

Billy knows the proper words to say, but they are not his, nor does he even have the authority to say them or to fold the flag or to give it to Meadows, who looks at the offered flag as though he does not understand what he is supposed to do with it.

"Kid," says Billy, "I don't know how grateful the nation is, or how much the president might regret your loss, but here's your country's flag. You put it somewhere and let it remind you of what your son must have felt in his heart."

Epilogue

THERE WAS A BREAKFAST, AFTER, catered by the local Safeway. Nothing fancy. Rolls and coffee and juice and fruit and some cheeses.

A young man, one of the high school friends, was going back to Manchester and said he'd be happy to carry Billy and me back there with him, right to the airport, where we were going to fly back to Norfolk. Meadows had found us a two-for-one deal on the Internet. But when we tried to work the machine at the airport that gives you your e-ticket, it just wouldn't go. We asked a woman behind the counter to figure it out for us. She checked it out and then said an e-ticket wasn't going to work for us. We didn't care what kind of ticket we had, we just wanted to get home. At least I did.

The woman got on the phone and said somebody would be by to help us. Why we needed special help was beyond me. She whispered that we were on the "No-Fly" list. Two men showed up and we showed them our driver's licenses. Don't know why

I still have one, Ruth drives me everywhere I have to go. They wanted our phone numbers too. Billy gave them the number off his new cell phone, read it right off the display for them. They wanted our social security numbers too. Well, I don't even know mine by heart, and Billy wasn't going to give them his number or anything else except his smart mouth. His style was hardly ingratiating, but the substance of what he said was not out of line: How did we get on this "No-Fly" list? (We had a pretty good idea.) Who makes up this list? What does it mean to be on it? How do we get off it? The answers to these questions and others were not forthcoming. We took the train.

All the way back to Dover, Delaware, and to Billy's car, this time making all the connections, we wondered about this list and about how many other lists there might be and what the chances were we'd be on those lists, too, and how here we were, free citizens of a free country, eighty-sixed from all flying machines. We fumed with rage, until we realized somewhere between Boston and New York that we didn't want to fly anywhere anyways, and then we laughed, cancelling imaginary vacations to Paris, France. We'd seen most of the world already, from the deck of one fighting ship or another, to the beach of one country or another, and we had no desire to see much more. But we went on laughing about missing next winter on the beaches of Aruba or the Mexican Riviera or Cuba, and on that one realized that even if they allowed us to fly they would not allow us to visit Cuba. Free citizens of a free country, free to go anywhere in the world that'll have us, with one exception: a small island country ninety miles from our coast, which happens to make, according to Billy, the finest cigars on the planet, and possibly the hottest women. I would trust him on the cigars.

We keep in touch by cell phone now. No more missions, no more escort TDY, no more chasing. They have an open invitation to my church and we have an open invitation to their bar, neither of which anyone seems to be making plans to accept. Yes, Meadows made the move to Norfolk and is pretty much in charge of things, and Billy is content to let him be. He was proud, Meadows was, to tell me that he refurbished the grille and they are once again putting out an honest hamburger from eleven a.m. to one a.m., and people are coming to the place just for the burgers.

The first week Meadows was living and working with Billy, he received a call from the Portsmouth bank where he had a checking account. Unbeknownst to him, his son had a safe deposit box at the same bank. They were calling to say that the government ordered the box opened and they wanted to send him its contents, a letter, which the government agent read but resealed.

When the letter arrived, he asked Billy to read it first and tell him then whether or not he should read it himself. Billy read it and told him he should. Later, he made a copy of it and sent it to me.

Dear Dad,

If you are reading this, then the worst has happened in our family. You've been notified that I have made the ultimate sacrifice in the service of my country. I was always prepared to make that sacrifice. I love my country, and if you love something you have to be ready to die defending it. I want you to understand that I am honored to die in this way, protecting the United States of

America. Please don't feel bad that my life was so short. It was a good life. I know you never wanted me to join the Marines, so I appreciate the way you supported me even so. You were the greatest father, and I love you. I'm with Mom now and we will both watch over you. Dad, please bury me in my uniform, next to Mom.

Your loving son, Larry

* * *

A good boy. A good son. A man of loyalty and courage and youthful idealism. We got it right somehow, we did what he wanted us to do. We know now what was in his heart. The heart of the man who sent this boy to his fate in a distant desert we will not likely ever know.